A Man Whose Business Is Death . . .

Slocum looked over his shoulder and saw his luck had run out. Throwing down on the revived shotgun-wielding man would result in death—the wrong one's death, from Slocum's point of view.

"Suppose I ought to talk to Hawkins."

"That's *Mister* Hawkins."

Slocum saw the man's finger curling back on the trigger and turning white with strain. He wasn't going to crawl for anyone. Something in the set to Mac's body—was it fear of disobeying Leonard Hawkins?—made Slocum relax just a little. When he stood, Mac motioned down the street with the muzzle of his shotgun. Aware that he might die at any instant in spite of the order to be brought in alive, Slocum set off. He saw how the townspeople hid. Fearful eyes peered out from around half-opened doors and through filmy curtains.

"Where are we going?"

"To the undertaker," Mac said.

JAKE LOGAN

SLOCUM
BURIED ALIVE

J
JOVE BOOKS, NEW YORK

THE BERKLEY PUBLISHING GROUP
Published by the Penguin Group
Penguin Group (USA) LLC
375 Hudson Street, New York, New York 10014

USA • Canada • UK • Ireland • Australia • New Zealand • India • South Africa • China

penguin.com

A Penguin Random House Company

SLOCUM BURIED ALIVE

A Jove Book / published by arrangement with the author

For information, address: The Berkley Publishing Group,
a division of Penguin Group (USA) LLC,
375 Hudson Street, New York, New York 10014.

ISBN: 978-0-515-15441-2

PUBLISHING HISTORY
Jove mass-market edition / June 2014

PRINTED IN THE UNITED STATES OF AMERICA

10 9 8 7 6 5 4 3 2 1

Cover illustration by Sergio Giovine.

1

Riding into the small town at the western edge of the Texas Hill Country, Espero by name if he could believe the sign with the chipped paint lettering a quarter mile back along the road to San Antonio, sent shivers up and down John Slocum's spine. He had ridden far enough and learned enough over the years to heed this silent feeling. Without being too obvious about it, he pushed back his battered tan canvas duster and flicked the leather thong off the Colt Navy's hammer. He kept riding to the Six Feet Under Saloon and actually considered not stepping down to go inside for a drink to wet his whistle.

The trail across Texas had been long, wet with summer rains, and boring. Once he had seen what might have been a few Comanches halfheartedly being chased by a cavalry patrol. Another time he had passed a stagecoach rattling along at a breakneck speed behind an eight-horse team. The look he had gotten from the shotgun messenger told him there wouldn't be any polite exchanges that day. He wondered if that put him on edge now. The driver and the guard on the stage had obviously been worried about road agents. He hadn't seen another rider the rest of the day—yesterday?

Pondering the matter, he nodded and mumbled to himself. It had been yesterday, even if it seemed years ago. That chance encounter had warned him of outlaws, and he must have carried that worry into Espero.

The townspeople milling about in the hot afternoon looked prosperous enough. No one in sight carried a six-shooter. That meant the law kept a tight lid on thievery and mayhem. If the marshal hadn't adhered strictly to the law, all the men would be packing side arms or hefting shotguns and rifles. Any lawman disarming the populace amid serious crime found himself out of a job or presiding over a ghost town. With so much of Texas vacant and waiting to be settled, it was easy to pull up stakes and move on until a more satisfactory town presented itself.

He looped the reins of his pinto through a rusty iron ring at the corner of the saloon, made sure the horse had enough lead to drink from a nearby water barrel, then went inside to satisfy his own thirst. Slocum stopped and looked around as he stepped into the cooler interior. Cigar smoke hung like fog inside. Only two men he saw puffed away but both worked furiously at their stogies. Clouds of blue-gray smoke wreathed them and hid their faces from sight, but he had no problem seeing what they were doing. Quick fingers shuffled a deck of cards and even more agile ones dealt seconds.

The two smokers had the look of tinhorn gamblers out to fleece the three others at the table with them. One player leaned so far to his right his partner had to prop him up. Another was so far in his cups that he peered across the table with one eye closed to keep perspective.

"You want to bet his hand, too?" the gambler next to the drunk cowpoke asked as he braced up his friend. Not a hint of sarcasm rang in those words. "I can help you figure the odds if you need."

"Jed's fine. Just a little under the weather today."

"Got a snootful of Horace's damned whiskey's what put him under. Lucky it don't put him six feet under."

The two gamblers laughed at this play on the saloon's name. Jed's eyes shot open in horror. He pushed back from the table and sat bolt upright.

"I ain't dead. You can't bury me. I'm not dead!" He looked around with such an expression of terror on his face that Slocum almost backed out of the saloon. Something about the suddenly sober man's fear fit together with his own apprehension about Espero.

"First one's on the house, mister, then you gotta pay," called Horace, the barkeep. The man held up an empty beer mug in one hand and a shot glass in the other. "What's your poison? Beer or whiskey? You won't find cheaper booze anywhere in South Texas, and that's a guarantee."

For once in his life, Slocum had plenty of money, almost ten dollars left over from a season of wrangling at a huge spread east of San Antonio. He moved into the room, the lumpy sawdust scuffing along with his dirty boots. With his elbows on the bar, he leaned forward so his hand could move under his duster and remain near his ebony-handled Colt.

"Free is good," he said.

"You got to pay for the second and I give you both at the same time."

"Fair enough," Slocum said, working around in his vest pocket with his left hand until his fingers teased out a dime. He dropped it on the counter, where it spun around on its rim, making a musical, silvery sound.

The barkeep's move was faster than a striking rattler. The coin disappeared, and hardly slower, two shot glasses of whiskey appeared in its place. To Slocum's surprise, the barkeep added two mugs of beer, as well.

"You weren't joshing about the dirt cheap prices here," Slocum said.

Instead of bragging on the Six Feet Under's policy, Horace grunted and moved away. Slocum didn't understand the reaction so he figured it must have been something he said. What that might have been was a true mystery since he was complimenting the barkeep on how he ran the saloon.

Slocum looked up into the mirror behind the bar and surveyed the crowd through the smoke. He had been in tougher drinking establishments than this, but the uneasy feeling persisted. During the war, he had learned to listen to this sixth sense. It had kept him alive over the years and up to this point, when he had just ridden into Espero and was given a free drink. And three cheap additional ones, to boot.

He stared into the murky amber fluid, then downed it in a single gulp. He took a half step back as it exploded in his mouth, burned his throat, and then turned into a raging fire in his belly. He shook his head to clear it.

"Best damn whiskey you'll find in town," the bartender said, edging back. He wiped his hands on his canvas apron, then twirled his long mustaches until they came to points sharper than the rowels on a Spanish vaquero's spurs. "I mix it up myself with a special formula I learned tendin' bar on a riverboat."

"This has brandy in it," Slocum said, his voice hoarse.

"You got a discerning taste, sir. I like customers who appreciate my mixing skills. What else is in it?"

Slocum rolled his tongue around his tormented mouth and caught the hint of red pepper. He told the barkeep this and added, "Might be a touch of nitric acid, too."

"Mister, you pose a real problem for me. Do I kill you—"

Slocum tensed, his hand moving closer to the butt of his pistol.

"Or do I hire you? You nailed it with all my special ingredients."

"Nails, too. Rusty nails to give it color," Slocum said.

"Now I simply have to hire you. That's the Gospel truth."

"If you don't mind, I'll poison myself again." Slocum took the second glass and knocked it back. This time the potent whiskey failed to deliver the mule's kick the first had.

"That's mighty good." With quick gulps, Slocum drained the beers to put out the raging fire in his belly. The bitter brew proved exactly what was needed to quell the effects of alcohol laced with acid and hot pepper.

"Another? Still cheap at twice the price." The barkeep held up the bottle, grinning enough to show a gold tooth, then his face sort of melted. He lowered the bottle and put it back under the bar and wiped his hands.

"I reckon another whiskey with a beer chaser would keep the others from getting too lonely," Slocum said, patting his belly.

The barkeep backed up wordlessly, then busied himself wiping away nonexistent spots on the already highly polished cherrywood bar. In spite of this faked concentration, he leaned slightly as if eavesdropping on a conversation Slocum wasn't having.

Slocum looked up into the mirror again and saw the reason for the barkeep's sudden change of mind. The man looked around, then turned and stared straight at Slocum so their eyes met in the mirror. He walked over slowly, giving Slocum plenty of time to size him up.

"You're the shootist that just rode into town." The words were cold, and it wasn't a question.

"No." Slocum swirled the remaining drops of amber beer around the bottom of the mug.

"Shootist and a liar," the man said.

"I'm not looking for a fight. Why are you?" Slocum shifted his elbows on the bar so his right hand moved closer to his cross-draw holster.

"He wants to hire you."

"That's mighty vague. Even if I was a gunslinger, I wouldn't be interested since I'm just passing through."

"Mr. Hawkins don't take 'no' for an answer. Ever."

"Do tell." Slocum knocked back the remnants of the second beer and spun about, smashing the mug into the center of the man's forehead.

The vessel shattered and shards slashed at weathered skin. Blood spewed forth, but the sudden attack had done as Slocum intended. The man had been pushing back his duster to lift a scattergun slung over his shoulder from a leather strap. The wound made him reach up with both hands, the shotgun forgotten.

Slocum grabbed the man by the shoulders and drove his knee into the man's groin. Air rushed from his lungs, and he made tiny mewling sounds as he sank to the sawdust-covered floor. Slocum gauged distances again and used his knee once more. This time he caught the man's chin and snapped his head back. With a loud crash, the man stretched out flat on his back, unconscious.

"Mister, you shouldna done that," Horace said. The barkeep had blanched whiter than a muslin sheet. "You don't rile Mr. Hawkins."

"I'm not a gunfighter, and I don't kill people for no reason. Or for pay." Slocum stepped over the fallen man, then looked back at the bartender. "Sometimes they give me a reason."

He went to the saloon doors and found himself staring down the muzzles of a half-dozen guns. Five of them trembled. One man held his six-shooter in both hands and even that didn't stop the shaking. The only one with a steady grip wore a shiny marshal's badge on his chest.

"Mister, you just made a whale of a mistake."

"Are you arresting me for defending myself? He was going to shoot me in the back with a shotgun."

"Mac wasn't gonna do any such thing. Leonard requested the honor of your presence, and you showed no civility at all. And I know Mac'd have asked you real nice. He's that sorta fellow."

"Leonard Hawkins?"

The marshal grinned crookedly.

"Good that you done heard of him. Can't imagine why you'd refuse his offer of a job."

"I don't know anybody in Espero," Slocum said carefully.

He discounted everyone but the marshal. Already some of the men's aims wavered. One even looked to have pissed himself and there hadn't been any gunplay. "The name *Hawkins* doesn't mean a thing to me."

"Come on along. I'll let Leonard tell you what he wants." The marshal snickered.

As he stepped back to usher Slocum ahead of him, the marshal gasped and bent double, holding his gut. Slocum knew it wasn't an excuse to shoot his hostage when he saw blood oozing out of the lawman's nose, dripping down to stain his vest. A quick step brought Slocum to the marshal's side and a quick blow with his elbow caught him in the diaphragm. The marshal dropped to the ground as much out of the fight as the man laid out inside the saloon.

"He needs a doctor. Why don't you all go fetch one?" When no one moved, Slocum snapped, "Now!" His years as a captain in the CSA had given him the voice required to motivate men who otherwise stood around too shocked by what they saw to act.

The five with the marshal scurried off like cockroaches in sudden daylight.

"You'd be a dead man right now if Mr. Hawkins hadn't asked to talk to you."

Slocum looked over his shoulder and saw his luck had run out. Throwing down on the revived shotgun-wielding man would result in death—the wrong one's death, from Slocum's point of view.

"Suppose I ought to talk to Hawkins."

"That's *Mister* Hawkins."

Slocum saw the man's finger curling back on the trigger and turning white with strain. He wasn't going to crawl for anyone. Something in the set to Mac's body—was it fear of disobeying Leonard Hawkins?—made Slocum relax just a little. When he stood, Mac motioned down the street with the muzzle of his shotgun. Aware that he might die at any instant in spite of the order to be brought in alive, Slocum set off. He saw how the townspeople hid. Fearful eyes peered out from around half-opened doors and through filmy curtains.

"Where are we going?"

"To the undertaker," Mac said.

Slocum considered this fitting. He was itching to resolve this standoff. If lead started flying, one of them would die. He looked for a watering trough or a wagon to use as shelter from the rain of lead pellets due to come his way. As luck would have it, Slocum saw nothing to protect him from gunfire, much less the discharge from a double-barreled shotgun.

"Go on in. He's waiting for you."

"*Mister* Hawkins?" Slocum asked. He put as much sarcasm into the question as he could, wanting a response from his captor.

"You—"

"That'll be enough, Mac." A portly man with muttonchops and a finely tailored suit that had to have cost a hundred dollars pushed open the door so Slocum could enter.

"Yes, sir," the shotgun-toting man said.

"You must be Leonard Hawkins," said Slocum.

"Uh, no, I'm not. I'm Kenneth Hawkins." He ran his fingers under his satin lapels and puffed up his chest. He looked back into the funeral parlor as if he was escaping, then pushed past Slocum.

For a moment, Slocum was alone. Kenneth Hawkins was gone and Mac had disappeared. He realized trying to hightail it only postponed returning to this very spot. The longer he dallied, the more likely somebody would die and provide a coffin with an occupant. He stepped inside and looked around the vestibule. Two fancy wooden caskets formed a short corridor. On the other side of each casket a varnished pine box offered a cheaper alternative more likely to be used by the average Espero citizen.

Slocum hesitated when soft music filtered through heavy dark maroon velvet curtains hiding the rear room. It came baleful and somber, fitting for a funeral parlor. Slocum had to find out whose funeral was being planned. His hand touched the ebony butt of his Colt, made sure the weapon slid easily from its holster, then pushed through the curtains into a room lit by a dozen black tapers. The flames guttered when the air from the outer room intruded and then steadied again as Slocum let the curtains softly sigh closed behind him.

The man seated to one side of the bier was the spitting image of Kenneth Hawkins. This had to be a brother.

This had to be Leonard Hawkins.

Slocum said nothing, keeping his eyes fixed on the man, who carefully dipped a steel-nibbed pen into an inkwell as he wrote a letter. When Hawkins was satisfied, he blew on the ink to dry it and then pushed the letter aside. Eyes so blue they were almost transparent fixed on Slocum. Hawkins's face was fleshy and round, matching his bulging belly and dangling wattles. Thin blond hair had been greased back severely, letting only a small cascade fall over his tiny ears as if to hide them. In spite of those ears being close to deformed in size, Slocum guessed they caught everything said, not only in the building but anywhere in town.

"So?" Hawkins asked.

"You should use a blotter to dry the ink."

The expression on the man's pudgy face defied description. Ripples flowed and his bloated lips curled back to show perfect teeth. Then he laughed.

"You are a peculiar man, sir."

"I don't like having a shotgun shoved into my spine."

"Do men usually end up dead when that happens?" Hawkins leaned forward in anticipation of Slocum's answer. When none came, the man nodded. "I see that it does. You carry yourself like a gunman, and the handle of your six-gun is worn."

"I'm not going to kill anyone for you, no matter what you offer. I'm not a paid murderer."

"But you have killed. I see it in your eyes. As owner of

the Hawkins Mortuary Service, in business for more than twenty years, I have seen every possible reaction to death. Some mourn in stoic silence, others cry openly, but those aren't what I look at. I look in the eyes. There I see tombstones or destroyed dreams. In your eyes I see the willingness to kill, but for a good and fair reason. Am I wrong?"

"What do you want?"

"What do I want? I can see you want nothing more than to be on your way, even if you have no clear idea where that might be. You are a drifter and ride for the setting sun or some other unattainable goal. Always restless, never satisfied, you will never find peace of mind."

"I'm feeling my boot heels telling me it's time to go wandering."

"Wait, don't go. My offer of temporary employment will be to our mutual advantage."

"I'm not looking for work."

"I will offer you five hundred dollars to escort my fiancée from Dexter Junction back here."

Slocum tried to remember the lay of the land. The distance between Dexter and Espero was only fifty miles. Three days in the saddle each way if he took it easy.

"Why don't you go fetch her yourself?"

"Alas, I am unable to do so." Hawkins thrust out his foot, wrapped in clean white bandages. "Gout makes even standing unbearable. And I would send my brother, but he is even more infirm."

"He looked fine to me when I ran into him outside your establishment."

"Kenneth? No, not him. Kenneth is the town banker. I meant Junior, the marshal."

"The marshal's your brother, too? This whole town related to you?"

"Of course not. I would send Junior, but the consumption he suffers is severe enough to keep him from horseback for any protracted journey."

"You'd pay me five hundred dollars to escort your bride-to-be? Nothing else?"

"Nothing more. One hundred in gold to seal the deal, the remainder when you deliver her safely into my loving arms."

"How will I recognize her?" Slocum damned himself for asking such a question. Hawkins was holding something back. Offering such a princely sum for an armed escort didn't ring true.

"Here is her picture. She is due on the train from Houston two days hence. You will greet her, then see her safely to Espero." Hawkins passed over a hand-tinted photograph of about the prettiest woman Slocum could remember seeing. The artist had lightly rouged her cheeks and reddened her lips. Her hair was a midnight black and her eyes, if the artist wasn't exaggerating with his talents, were so blue the very sky would cry in envy.

Slocum started to return it, but Hawkins waved it off. Slocum saw that the undertaker's fingers were all adorned with gold and silver rings, some with diamonds inset. The dying trade in Espero paid well.

"Keep it for reference."

"What'll keep me from taking your money and never fetching her back?"

From behind came the hushed sound of the curtains opening.

"Mac will see to that." Hawkins leaned back and opened a drawer in his writing desk, took out a small leather bag, and tossed it to Slocum. From the way it jingled, the gold coins were inside.

Slocum tucked it away in his coat pocket.

Hawkins lifted his almost-invisible eyebrows in surprise.

"Aren't you going to count it?"

"When I get back," Slocum said.

This brought a frown to the undertaker's face, then he smiled and waved Slocum away as if he were a menial.

"Best get on the trail. You will not keep Miss Madison waiting."

Slocum turned and stared at the mountain of a man who would be his unwanted trail companion. He doubted Mac would be as easy to deck a second time. If trouble brewed, lead would fly.

Which had to be exactly what Leonard Hawkins feared or he wouldn't have sought out a man he thought to be a gunman to escort his fiancée back to Espero.

2

"You don't talk much," Mac said after they'd been on the trail for more than an hour.

Slocum glanced over at him. It had taken the better part of twenty minutes to figure out why Leonard Hawkins had sent the pair of them rather than dispatching Mac alone to pick up Miss Madison. Hawkins had a suspicious mind and probably didn't trust one man to be alone with the girl, though why he hadn't found another citizen in Espero to take this trip was something of a poser. Even if the marshal was laid up and the banker wasn't up to the trip, there had to be more than Mac willing to go.

Five hundred dollars was a mighty big pile of money to offer a stranger, too. That made Slocum suspicious of ever collecting. There hadn't been any point in opening the leather bag and counting the coins. Somehow Slocum sensed that Hawkins had expected him to do just that—and the lack of faith would have pleased the undertaker. What secret thrill he got from meeting those expectations, or maybe smashing ones that didn't include him being a generous son

13

of a bitch, lay beyond Slocum's reckoning. Leonard Hawkins was a tricky bastard who never laid all his cards on the table.

Or maybe the cards worth looking at were up his sleeve.

"You work long for Hawkins?"

"Knew the cat hadn't got your tongue. Yeah, worked for him going on a year now."

"That's not so long."

"It is in Espero. Nobody wants to stay in that town. The ranches all around town barely keep it alive. The railroad went to Dexter Junction, and that caused Espero to dry up. It's only waiting for a strong wind to finish blowing it away."

"Not that Hawkins cares a whit about the living since dying is his business," Slocum said.

Mac's reaction put him on his guard.

"What have you heard about Mr. Hawkins?"

"Nary a thing. I just rode into town and had just knocked back two shots of that snake piss the barkeep called whiskey when you came in."

"He saw you ride in and knew you was the one."

"How come he doesn't trust you to escort the girl?"

"There's—" Mac cut off whatever he intended to say. "We been having problems with road agents. Two guns are better 'n one along this stretch of the road."

Whatever the real reason, Mac wasn't about to spit it out.

"You want to show me that picture again?" Mac had taken Miss Madison's picture from him and tucked it into his vest pocket before Slocum had a chance to do more than marvel at her good looks. "Or does he want that kept from me, too?"

"He's not keeping anything from you. It's just like he said. We escort Miss Madison back to Espero, and him and her'll get hitched. He's sent for the preacher man already. He rides a circuit, and it takes a couple weeks for him to come around usually."

There hadn't been a church anywhere Slocum had seen in town, but he hadn't been looking. Not for a church. The only communing he wanted to do was with a bottle, a meal, and maybe a willing woman. Hawkins had pretty much removed all three of those things from his horizon, forcing Slocum to live with the memory of the strong liquor served up at the Six Feet Under Saloon.

Slocum resisted the temptation to count the money in the bag. Nothing about going to Dexter Junction set well with him. If Hawkins had given him money, riding off with it wouldn't bruise his conscience one little bit. He didn't like having men point guns at him for no reason. He had been dragooned into this trip when he ought to have volunteered. Most of all, Mac's presence bothered him. The shotgun remained slung under the big man's right arm, ready to be spun out and used.

"How'd he come to meet Miss Madison?"

"They haven't met yet."

Slocum nodded. Mail-order brides weren't all that unusual. Women back East got tired of hunting for husbands and saw nothing wrong with marrying sight unseen some gent out West. Hawkins's situation looked to be better than most. The undertaker had plenty of money if he threw it around hiring a man like Slocum to fetch his bride. The rings and other jewelry he wore hinted at a fraction of the man's riches. With a brother working as town marshal and another running the bank, Leonard Hawkins damned near owned Espero.

His thoughts wandered down that path. Was that why no one else in town could be trusted to escort the man's bride back to Espero? Bankers and marshals weren't among the most liked. An undertaker thrown into that mix might make the entire Hawkins clan men to be feared.

"She's a mighty fine-looking woman," Slocum said.

"Don't you go getting any ideas," Mac snapped.

"I didn't mean anything by it," Slocum said. He wasn't the marrying kind. He once had a girlfriend back in Calhoun, Georgia, but that had been before he had marched off to war with his brother, Robert.

Robert had been killed in Pickett's Charge at the Angle,

and years later Slocum had gotten himself gut-shot by Bloody Bill Anderson after complaining to Quantrill about the brutality of the raid on Lawrence, Kansas. He had crept back to Slocum's Stand to recuperate. His ma and pa had died, his brother was buried in some unmarked Virginia grave, and a carpetbagger judge had taken a shine to the farm. A man can take only so much.

Slocum had left the judge and his hired gun buried down by the springhouse and had ridden westward, never looking back. What with a reward on his head for killing a Federal judge, even a Reconstruction judge, he had never lingered long in any one place. Riding suited him just fine since most towns bored him after a day or a week. Some jobs he'd kept longer. Punching cattle suited him. A season on the range was tolerable. Even gambling proved a profession he could tolerate, though most towns ran gamblers out if they had a suspicious winning streak. Depending on the town, that might mean as little as being fifty dollars ahead.

Mostly Slocum rode, not looking for trouble but not running away like a scalded dog when it happened to find him.

Like now.

"I'll talk to her when we get to Dexter," Mac said. He put his hand over the pocket holding the picture. "All I got to do is match this up and—"

He sat straighter in the saddle, then looked down at the hand clamped over his heart. A tiny red circle spread. Mac pulled his hand away. The red spread like wildfire on his chest. He looked up, confused, then grated out, "I been shot."

He toppled from the saddle, a giant tree sawed down. He hit the ground with a thud and never moved.

Slocum reached for his six-shooter, but he hesitated to draw. He hadn't heard a rifle's report, yet there was no denying how Mac had died. A quick look ahead showed how the road curved to the left after entering a thicket. A sniper hiding there had a straight shot, and the rifle report might have been muffled by the vegetation.

When a glint of sunlight off the rifle barrel showed, Slocum bent low over his horse's neck and put his heels to straining flanks. He rocketed off the road and into a jumble of undergrowth almost too dense for the horse to plow through. Slocum kicked free of the stirrups, hit the ground, and yanked his Winchester from the saddle sheath. As he moved back toward the road, he levered in a round. By the time he got a good view ahead along the road, the sniper had disappeared.

Slocum settled down and braced his rifle against a tree trunk. During the war he had been a sniper and a good one. He had learned patience sitting in the crotch of a tree for long hours, waiting for the single flash of sunlight off Yankee braid. Cutting off the head by killing the officer left the blue beast to thrash about in confusion. More than one battle had been turned because of his marksmanship. More than accuracy, he had learned patience.

This time, the forbearance wore on him. He drew back his rifle and made his way through the thicket, paralleling the road. The shot had come from more than seventy-five yards. A good shot but not one impossible for even a fair marksman. Mac had been a huge target, and hitting him smack in the heart could have been pure luck.

Slocum slowed and fought his way through the brambles as he approached the spot where the killer had lain in wait. Movement in the brush put him on alert. He lifted his rifle, then lowered it and fired almost point blank as a javelina snorted, then let out a piggish squeal of rage as it charged him. His slug ripped off a portion of the hog's shoulder. It thundered on. He didn't have time to work the lever. The pig crashed into him, knocking him over. More by instinct than planning, Slocum swung the rifle and drove the stock into the wounded animal's head. He knocked it away.

Rolling in the other direction, he whipped out his six-shooter. The javelina's tiny eyes squinted down in pure animal fury. It pawed at the ground like a bull ready to charge.

This small hesitation gave Slocum time to get off one round, a second, and then a third. The hog exploded forward. Slocum triggered the final three rounds as the heavy animal smashed into him. Again he went tumbling, but this time the pig's snout with the vicious curved tusks stopped only inches from his face. Saliva dripped down those yellowed teeth and onto his duster.

With a mighty heave, Slocum threw the dead pig off him, then stood, panting. He realized he made a perfect target for whoever had gunned down Mac. Reloading as fast as he could, he picked up his rifle and went hunting.

It took only a few seconds for him to find the spot in the thicket where the sniper had drawn his deadly bead. From the evidence there had been two men here, and the javelina's tracks showed why they hadn't stuck around to put Slocum into a grave the way they had Mac. The pig had come for them, frightening them off.

Slocum counted himself as lucky on several scores. They had shot Mac and not him, then the javelina had driven them from a secure position, and finally Lady Luck had downright smiled on him. Otherwise the javelina would have ripped him to bloody shreds. Instead, he had killed it and not taken any damage other than pig spit and some blood on his coat.

Rather than tempt fate, Slocum returned to where Mac lay in the hot sun drawing flies, making his way through the undergrowth rather than exposing his back on the road. When he reached the fallen man, he stared at him. Mac's death changed everything. He could ride away, and it would be days before Hawkins figured out he wasn't returning with his bride.

Slocum rolled Mac over, pried free the vest pocket matted with blood, and worried out the woman's picture. He smiled ruefully. The bullet had cut out most of her face. The dried blood on the picture had turned it brittle. He started to toss it away, then looked at it, remembering the shy smile that had been blown away, the tipped-in blue eyes, and the lovely face. He tucked the picture into his own vest pocket, then rummaged through the dead man's pockets. Mac had less than a dollar in small change. There wasn't even a watch.

Digging a grave in the soft earth was easy, but Slocum knew burying Mac deep enough to keep the animals from digging up the grave for a quick meal wasn't in the cards. Returning to Espero and letting the man's employer tend to the burial fleetingly passed through his mind, but Slocum decided on a different course of action.

He had been hired to escort the woman back to her betrothed. He didn't owe anything to Mac or Leonard Hawkins, but letting her stand on the railroad platform, all forlorn and wondering what was going on, wasn't to be endured. Of all the things Slocum had done to keep him awake at night, *that* wasn't going to be another.

He finished the burial, then mounted and continued down the road, warily looking for the snipers. Mac's horse trailed behind, giving him a spare to switch to when his pinto flagged.

He reached Dexter Junction hours before the train arrived.

Slocum sat in the shade, his hat brim pulled low to further shield his eyes as he squinted into the morning sun. The train from Houston was due in anytime. He checked his pocket watch a half-dozen times before the depot agent called out to him, "The train'll get here when it gets here. You ain't speedin' it up none lookin' at the time every couple minutes."

Slocum snapped the lid shut and tucked the watch away. The agent was right. He wanted to deliver Miss Madison to Espero and be on his way. Being anxious only made the time crawl by. He leaned back and tried to figure out what Hawkins's response to learning of Mac's death might be. Getting his bride all safe and sound might ease the bad news, but Slocum doubted it. His best course of action was to

escort Miss Madison to the edge of Espero and let her pro-
ceed on her own to tell Hawkins about his employee's death.

Then again, Slocum might send her on into town and
never tell her there had been a second escort. Either way, he
lost four hundred dollars. He fumbled out the bag from his
pocket and for the first time unknotted the leather string and
poured the contents into his left palm. The five tiny twenty-
dollar gold coins sparkled in the light. Hawkins had played
fair with him.

So far.

That niggling thought returned that the undertaker was
crookeder than a dog's hind leg, though Slocum had no proof
of that.

"There she is, mister. See the steam from the smoke-
stack?"

At the depot agent's alert, he looked up at the same time
a loud whistle blast reached across the half mile loud enough
to make Slocum flinch. He put the coins back into his
pocket, then tossed the leather bag away and stood, waiting
for the train.

It chuffed and whistled and finally screeched to a halt at
the platform. The locomotive pulled a half-dozen passenger
cars and several freight cars. Stepping back, Slocum saw a
mail car and finally a caboose. He walked down the length
of the platform as passengers began stepping off. Studying
each for any sign of the woman caused a bit of panic to rise.

Miss Madison wasn't among the passengers leaving. He
caught a conductor's arm and asked, "Was there a woman
aboard?"

The conductor looked at him as if he had been out in the
sun too long.

"Mistah, there's a whole passel o' wimmen what been
ridin' this heah train."

Slocum started to pull out the photograph, then remembered how little use it would be in identifying Miss
Madison.

"She's not gotten off. Mind if I look in the cars?"

"Hep yo'sef, but if 'n you stays aboard, you buy a ticket to Eagle Pass."

Slocum wondered if that wasn't the smartest thing he could do, then pushed the notion of leaving from his mind. He grabbed a handhold and pulled himself up onto the small metal platform and peered into the first passenger car. Seeing no one, Slocum went in and hurried the length to get to the next car and then the third. Before entering this car, he stopped and peered through the dirty window.

A woman stood with her back to him, talking to a man. They were pressed close, and Slocum thought they would kiss, but she pushed him away and turned toward the front of the car. Slocum entered the car and called out, "Miss Madison?"

She jumped as if he had stuck her with a pin.

"Why, yes. Who are you? You're not Leonard Hawkins."

"He sent me to escort you to Espero," Slocum said. He craned his neck to get a look at the man leaving the rear of the car but saw nothing more than the back of a head with sweat-matted hair.

"Nothing's wrong, is it?" She looked frightened and put her hand to her mouth. "Leonard should have come for me himself."

"He's laid up or he'd've come. Nothing to worry your head on. He'll explain everything in Espero. That's a couple days' travel. I'll get a buggy for us." He looked down. "That your only luggage?"

"Why, yes," she said uneasily.

"You do travel light." He picked up the case. It proved heavier than he'd expected, but it was the woman's only luggage.

"He's not here?"

"In Dexter Junction? He's fifty miles off in Espero," Slocum said. "You look surprised at that."

"Why, yes, I . . . I thought I was to meet him here. I didn't realize he was so far off."

"Reckon you're anxious to meet the man you're going to marry."

"I hadn't thought I'd have to travel." She looked around. For a moment, Slocum considered pulling out the picture to match it up with the reality of her face, but he left the photograph in his pocket. The bullet hole through the center would only agitate her further.

As he escorted her from the train, he wondered what else Hawkins hadn't told her.

And what else the undertaker hadn't bothered to tell him.

3

"One moment," the dark-haired beauty said, pulling away from him. She looked squarely at Slocum and studied him closely. "How do I know Leonard sent you?"

"You don't."

"Why should I go with you, then?"

"No reason other than I'm a man of my word, and I say Leonard Hawkins sent me to escort you to him in Espero."

"I don't know you."

"Have a good trip, Miss Madison. Most anyone in Dexter Junction can tell you how to get to Espero," Slocum said, tipping his hat. He walked off, not caring if she stopped him or not. Hawkins had drawn him into a chore that could have been delightful.

The woman was certainly pretty. Even after traveling halfway across southern Texas, she was a flower without compare. Escorting her to Espero could have been pleasant, except that Mac had been gunned down, and Slocum had no idea why the man had died. Mac hadn't seemed the sort to go through life without making enemies, including those willing to cut him down from ambush. As true as that might have been, Slocum had the gut feeling the murder tied in with picking up Miss Madison.

He was better off without the burden of knowing the motive for Mac's killing or why such a desirable woman had become a mail-order bride. A filly that good looking could have had her pick of men in Houston, rich ones, ones who could bury even a wealthy hombre like Leonard Hawkins under a pile of gold coins. She hadn't had any trouble striking up an acquaintance with the man on the train, even if he had turned tail and run off the instant the train stopped at the depot.

"Sir, wait. Wait!"

Slocum groaned. He had been afraid the woman would come to her senses. Without a friend in Dexter and no easy way to get to Espero, she had to rely on his goodwill.

"Is there a stagecoach from this town to, uh, Espero, where you said Leonard waits for me?"

"No stage," Slocum said, "as far as I know. I'm a stranger in these parts. I can ask and see you on the stagecoach, if those are your druthers."

"Why, uh, yes, yes, it is." She stood primly on the platform, her single case at her feet.

Slocum went to the ticket agent and asked after a stage.

"Ain't got one goin' there no more," the man said, pushing back his green eye shades. He wiped some ink from his hand on a filthy apron. "When the railroad came through, it well nigh killed the stagecoach company. They folded their tents and crept off into the night without payin' the feed bill or much else."

"The only way to reach Espero is on horseback?"

"If that's the way you want to travel." The agent leaned to peer past Slocum at the woman. "You can get a buggy over at the livery. Won't cost more 'n fifty–sixty dollars."

Slocum involuntarily touched his pocket, where Hawkins's money rested. If he paid that much for a buggy, he wouldn't have much left from the initial payment. His mind rolled over the possibilities. If he took her back, he stood a chance of collecting the other four hundred promised dollars, no matter that Mac had been gunned down. Hawkins wouldn't be happy, but if Slocum delivered his bride safe and sound, Mac's death might not matter that much.

He had to remind himself that Hawkins dealt with death and made money from it. If no one in Espero died, there wouldn't be any funerals.

Slocum thanked the agent and asked what the woman wanted to do. She chewed at her lower lip and looked around. The train vented a long, loud whistle that made her jump. Somehow she ended up in Slocum's arms. He noticed how well they fit together before she pushed herself away and watched the train pull out. They were alone on the platform now. In less than a minute the train vanished around a bend on its way to Eagle Pass on the Mexican border.

"I must place myself in your hands, sir," she said.

"Slocum," he said. "John Slocum." It took her a moment to understand what he said.

"Oh, your name. You already know me. Miranda Madison." She held out her hand, palm down as if she expected him to kiss it.

He took it in his huge hand and shook, being sure not to crush the fingers. She withdrew and looked a little sick at having touched him.

"Something wrong, ma'am?"

"You, uh, how do I say this politely? You smell like some wild animal."

"A horse," Slocum said. "I've been in the saddle for the past two days to get here." He had been astride his horse much longer than that and couldn't remember his last bath.

"Do I have to ride in such a fashion?"

Slocum considered what to tell her. Mac's horse had a saddle, and letting her ride would make the trip faster and cheaper for him if he didn't have to buy a buggy.

"Do you think Mr. Hawkins would repay me if I bought a buggy?"

"What was his plan for transporting me from here to, uh, Espero?" She looked around, lost. "Wherever Espero is."

Slocum hadn't asked and had thought Mac knew such details.

"I've got a spare horse. Let me see to getting a buggy for the trip. I can get some grub, too, since trail rations might not set well with you."

"I am tougher than I appear, sir," she said indignantly.

Slocum left her on the platform and spent the next hour haggling over the buggy, which set him back half his poke. A decent supply of food for the trip cost him another ten dollars, but Mac's horse took to the harness as if it was used to pulling rather than being ridden. Slocum settled in, snapped the reins, and got the flimsy buggy rolling through the potholed main street of Dexter Junction. He rounded a corner and drove straight for the railroad depot.

As he pulled up, he saw the man Miranda Madison had spoken with on the train jump from the platform and dash across the tracks, heading for the storage sheds.

"That man bothering you, Miss Madison?"

"What? Why, no. He's just someone I spoke to on the train."

"He lit out like someone'd set fire to his ass."

"Sir!"

She protested, but Slocum doubted such mild profanity offended her at all. She had the appearance of a hothouse flower, but he sensed a toughness to her that Hawkins might have a hard time accepting.

He took her case and stowed it amid the supplies, then helped her into the buggy.

"You don't have both horses hitched up?"

Slocum had tied his to the rear of the buggy. He knew from experience that the horse refused to pull in harness. The pinto was a saddle horse through and through. With a quick snap of the reins, he got Mac's horse to pulling through town and out onto the road back to Espero.

"This is such wild country," Miranda said, staring at the thick undergrowth amid the trees. "Those brambles could cut a person apart. They look as if they would leap from the forest and engulf the road in nothing flat if no one traveled here."

"This is the Hill Country. Things grow fast. You're likely right about the bramble bushes clogging up the road without constant traffic along it."

He stared ahead as he drove, alert for any hint of an ambush. In places the vegetation closed in on either side until reaching out would let him drag his hands through thorny plants. The buggy was light enough to be upset if a javelina attacked. A three-hundred-pound pig weighed more than the buggy. If the horse spooked, they could be left to the tusked fury of an angry pig.

"You lived in Houston all your life?" Slocum asked.

"What? Houston? Oh, no, I came from Chicago. I made my way down the Mississippi to New Orleans, then from there took a ship hugging the Texas coast. That's how I came to Texas."

"Your marriage prospects must have been better in Chicago or New Orleans—or even Houston. What made you answer an ad from Hawkins?"

"He answered my ad, Mr. Slocum. And my life has not been all beer and skittles, not at all."

He looked at her curiously.

"The only time I ever heard anyone say that, it was a remittance man from Manchester."

"Oh, I picked up all manner of odd phrases while floating down the river." She made an airy motion with her hand, dismissing the topic.

"Does your family know you advertised for a husband?"

"You are remarkably nosy, Mr. Slocum. My business is mine—and my future husband's. The truth is, my family died of cholera. I avoided coming down with the disease, but it left me adrift in a world I hardly understand. My letters from Leonard have shown him to be worldly-wise and a caring man." She hesitated, then asked almost timidly, "Is he as rich as he claims?"

"I don't know how rich he claimed to be, but he is certainly well off. Planting people pays well."

"I don't understand. 'Planting people'?"

"He's the town undertaker, but he's rich enough. His brother's the bank president and his youngest is town marshal."

"He is related to a lawman? Tell me more about the marshal."

That surprised Slocum. She was more interested in Junior Hawkins than his oldest brother.

"I can't say I know him. He's got an ailment that kept him from coming to fetch you. Could be that consumption doubles him up in pain." Slocum snorted and added in spite, "Junior doesn't strike me as the sharpest pencil on the teacher's desk."

Miranda's reaction made him wonder even more. Declaring Junior Hawkins to be a tad on the simple side let her relax visibly. She had been worrying at her linen handkerchief, running fingers along the lace patterns, and now she tucked it away in her left sleeve. For the first time since leaving the train station, she flashed him a genuine smile.

"It's good to know about my betrothed's family . . . before I meet them."

"You're marrying into the family, but you're marrying Leonard," Slocum said.

"An undertaker," she mused. "He hadn't mentioned that."

"Some folks might find that occupation disagreeable. He might not have wanted to scare off such a lovely woman."

"You think I'm pretty? Why, thank you, John. That's kind of you to say so." She trained those bright blue eyes on him, studying him intently now. "You're quite handsome yourself, if you'd take a bath and cut that shaggy hair."

"Here we are, just met, and already you're trying to make me over."

Miranda took it as a joke rather than a criticism and laughed in delight.

"I am going to enjoy this trip more than I thought."

"You only learned of it a few hours back," Slocum said. "You thought Hawkins was in Dexter Junction, not fifty miles down the road."

"Too bad it's not farther." She looked sharply at him when he reacted. "I mean the weather is superb and the road is clear. The journey is a grand adventure for me."

Slocum wondered how this was possible for a woman who had traveled the breadth of the country by herself to end up in a tiny Texas ranching town in the middle of nowhere. Her sidelong look at him made Slocum wonder if she judged his reaction to what was likely an outrageous claim.

He had no time to respond. The buggy took a sharp turn in the road. On either side, close in, the vegetation cut off escape. Ahead in the road were two road agents with bandannas pulled up over their faces and rifles leveled.

"Oh, John, what are you going to do?"

Miranda clutched at his arm. He jerked free and went for his six-shooter at the same time the two outlaws opened fire. The first slug missed him by a country mile. The second cut the crown of his Stetson.

"Damnation, that hat cost me a week's pay."

Miranda sputtered and tried to pull something from her clutch purse. Slocum half stood and interposed his body between her and the two mounted outlaws. With careful shooting, he spooked one man's horse, causing it to rear. He had hoped to see the outlaw thrown, but the horse turned and blundered into the other skittish animal. For a moment, Slocum thought they would go down together and give him a decent shot at their riders.

The smaller of the two expertly jerked at the reins and kept control. This let the rearing horse settle down.

"John, shoot them!"

He braced his gun hand against the buggy and squeezed off the most accurate shot possible. The nearer rider jerked and clutched at his thigh. Better yet, he dropped his rifle. Another shot set the pair to fleeing.

"You did it, you chased them off!" Miranda settled down. In a much calmer voice asked, "Who were they? Just common thieves?"

"Could be," Slocum allowed, but he doubted that. The coincidence of being stopped both ways along the road were too great.

"Are there so many road agents?"

"These parts aren't safe," Slocum said.

He settled down and reloaded. As he did, he ran the memory of every shot, every twitch, every rearing horse over in his head. The man who had dropped the rifle had been the sniper killing Mac on the way to Dexter. But the other? The man was smaller. Tiny clues came to Slocum through the flapping duster, pulled-down hat brim, and bandanna hiding the face. The second road agent was likely a woman. Whatever the two wanted, robbery hardly seemed to fit the bill.

With a snap on the reins, Slocum drove forward slowly until he came to the fallen rifle. He bent low, scooped it up, and looked at it.

"That's fancy etching on the receiver," Miranda said. "The outlaw is sure to want that back. I mean, he must have stolen it and would want to steal it back from you."

"All he has to do is ask me for it," Slocum said, sliding the rifle behind the buggy seat. "I'll give it back one bullet at a time."

"You are a violent man, John."

From her tone he tried to figure out if that appealed to her. Killing wasn't something he went out of his way to do, but if it came down to losing his own life or taking another, he had no qualms about pulling his Colt Navy's trigger as many times as it took. Since he had signed on to protect

Miranda Madison, however reluctantly, a couple more trigger pulls protected her, too.

"We ought to camp soon," he said. "Sun's dipping low, and it'll be too dangerous to keep driving at night."

"We shouldn't stop. Those road agents won't run far and will return to rob us. Or kill us."

"The horse isn't up to pulling the buggy much longer, and mine is only saddle broke. He doesn't take to harness at all."

"Very well."

He stared at her, wondering at the sudden change of mind. As he swung around another sharp turn, he cast a quick look back along the road and thought he spotted a rider. The outlaws boxed them in if he stayed on the road. The first double ruts he came to looked uninviting, weeds slapping wetly at the wheels and threatening to wrap around the axle.

Miranda sneezed and daintily wiped her nose with the lace-trimmed hanky stuffed up her sleeve.

"Goldenrod," Slocum said. "And there's an abandoned farmhouse."

"Driving through the weeds causes a yellow cloud to rise up." She sneezed again, as loud as a gunshot. "Please forgive me for being so unladylike."

Slocum snorted at that. She was headed for a town passed over by the railroad to marry the undertaker. Society events in Espero weren't going to be more than a church social, and Slocum hadn't even seen a church there.

"I'll check out the house," he said, fastening the reins around the buggy frame. He waited until he was just inside before drawing his six-shooter so Miranda wouldn't see how edgy he was. A quick look around showed the only life to be small, furry, and scuttling away. "Come on in," he called.

"Oh, my," she said. "I have stayed in nicer places." She sneezed, then added, "Worse, too. The trip from Chicago wasn't always first cabin."

He left her busily swiping at the debris, trying to find a

clean spot to lie down. He led the horses to a ramshackle barn and prowled about hunting for sign of a wolf or cougar making its den inside. The place was too dilapidated for such discerning creatures. He put the horses into stalls and tended them the best he could, then returned to the house. Wood remained in a pile behind the house. He hefted a couple logs and carried them inside to the fireplace.

"I brought in the supplies," Miranda said. "I'm not much of a cook but think I can whip up something. You chose well."

"It's not the first time I've been on the trail."

She looked at him. A tiny smile curled the corner of her lips and a twinkle came to her bright blue eyes.

"Nor, I suspect, the first time you've been on the trail alone with a woman."

"You're partly wrong," he said.

"What?" Miranda recoiled and straightened.

"I've never been on the trail with one so lovely."

She laughed, dabbed at her nose, and then said, "My, my, aren't we the Southern gentleman?" Bustling about, she began baking biscuits and arranging the rest to see what sort of meal she could whip up.

"I'll fetch more water," he said.

"I suppose I did wrong using what you had in the canteens."

"Nothing to bother yourself over," Slocum said. "I'll see if the pump still works."

He took the canteens and went outside to the well. The sun had about finished for the day, and bugs whined all around as he gripped the pump handle and began working it. The sucker washer down below had dried out. Without water to wet the seal, he doubted he had much chance of getting water up, if there was even any in the well. But he kept pumping and eventually a rush of water rewarded his efforts. He filled both canteens and started back into the house when he heard sounds beyond the barn.

Canting his head to one side, he listened hard. Someone moving about became unmistakable amid the drone of the insects.

Slocum rushed back to the house and called, "We've got company. Stay here while I . . ."

His words trailed off when he realized Miranda wasn't inside. Putting the canteens down, he drew his six-shooter and began to explore. He homed in on the distant sound, then froze when he heard a loud sneeze. Slocum turned in that direction. It was away from the disturbance he had already located.

Steps slow but steady, he went toward the distant trees where he had heard the sneeze—Miranda? It seemed likely.

The woods swallowed him whole and left him blind. Not a glimmer showed through the dense foliage. Making his way slowly now, he moved as quietly as possible. It wasn't silent enough.

A rustle from behind caused Slocum to spin around and go into a gunfighter's crouch, his six-shooter pointed at . . . nothing.

Then a heavy body fell from the tree limb above and the darkness became even more intense as he was knocked unconscious.

4

Slocum knew he wasn't dead. Death couldn't hurt this much. His head threatened to explode as his eyes bulged out and his ears felt as if someone had rammed an icepick through them. He rubbed the knot on his head. As scary as it was, if he hadn't worn his hat, he would have been in worse condition. The Stetson had cushioned most of the blow.

He pushed the hat away and gently probed. The pain sent lightning lancing through his head all the way down to his belly, making him sick. He rolled onto his side and retched weakly. After this he felt better.

And angrier.

He squeezed his eyes shut as tightly as possible, then opened them to a different world, one of grays and fleeting shadows rather than intense blackness. The shape of his six-gun drew him. The hard butt fit nicely into his grip. This more than anything else made him feel better as he braced himself against a sweet gum tree and pulled himself to his feet. A few seconds of wobbling passed. Slocum pushed his way through the thicket until he caught sight of the house.

The light from the fireplace caused shadows to move

about inside, but the erratic movement told him no human made those dark patches. He skirted the house, hunting for the man who had dropped from the tree and slugged him. Gunfire from the direction of the sounds that had alerted him at first echoed and died quickly, swallowed by the dense vegetation.

He made his way in that direction, then used the barn as shelter to peer about. A rider approached, hunched over the horse's neck. When the horse came within a few yards, the rider toppled to the ground, rolled over, moaned, and lay still. Slocum grabbed for the reins and almost had his arm jerked from the socket. He dug in his heels and brought the horse around. Holding the reins down low prevented it from rearing and using its hooves on him.

In his condition, a single hoof blow would have killed him.

He calmed the horse, then tied the reins to a rusted plow handle. Only then did he go to the fallen rider.

"Help him. Th-They got Frank, too!"

He grabbed the man's collar and jerked him to a sitting position. The loose clothing almost came off over the man's head—the *woman's* head. Her hat fell off, letting shoulder-length hair cascade down. The duster and coat she wore were a better fit on a man Slocum's height and weight, not a woman who weighed no more than a hundred pounds. As he pulled her to her feet, he saw she was a full foot shorter than his six feet.

The effect of the fall wore off. She began struggling in his grip and almost got away when she skinned out of the duster and the coat beneath. Slocum changed his grip and caught the front of her shirt. It tore away as she fought him, giving a flash of white skin and the valley between her small, pert breasts.

"Lemme go. You let me go!"

"You were begging me for my help a couple seconds ago."

"I didn't know who you were then."

"You do now?" Slocum caught his breath. He had more

than one wanted poster dogging his heels. Some were for minor offenses, but others, like the judge killing, meant his head in a noose if he got caught. "How do you know me?"

"You work for *him*. You're Hawkins's lapdog. He whistles and you come running."

While Slocum puzzled over that, the woman quieted and again gave him more to think about than he wanted.

"We can swap. Me for them. Me for the three of them. Please, mister, he'll like that, the son of a bitch!"

"I don't know what you're talking about."

"Like hell you don't. I saw you with McIntyre."

"You shot him?"

"Frank did. Frank's a damned good shot."

"So you've got a feud going with Leonard Hawkins?"

"A feud? Is that what he calls it? A feud! It's out-right war!"

Slocum wasn't ready for her to attack him with her balled-up hands. The bony fists hit and hurt. He ignored her until she started clawing for his eyes. His larger hand captured both her slender wrists and held them together, then he lifted until she was up on her toes. This way she could neither hit nor kick him.

That didn't keep her from trying. Slocum swung her around until she grunted in pain.

"Go on, do what you want with me. Only let Frank go. And . . . and my ma and pa, too!"

Slocum released her so suddenly she collapsed. On hands and knees, she glared up at him.

"I don't know what the hell you're talking about. If you've got a beef with Hawkins, that's your concern. Where's the woman from the cabin?"

"Hawkins's bitch? The one you were taking to him?"

Slocum said nothing. The woman could either vent her fury or simmer down.

"I don't know. We would have snatched her if we could have, but your boys ambushed us."

"After you took a few shots at me out on the road?"

"Yeah." She turned more sullen. This put Slocum on guard. When she tried to tackle him, he sidestepped and shoved her facedown on the ground. "Stop, I'm suffocating."

He barely heard her complaint since she had a mouthful of dirt. Warily releasing her, he dropped to the ground cross-legged in front of her as she spat dirt. Her glare turned even hotter.

"I don't know anything about kidnapping Frank."

"And I don't know a damned thing about you losing that fancy whore!"

"Might be we have the same problem, only dressed up in different clothing. The men who took Frank—he your husband?"

"My brother. All the family I have left after Hawkins grabbed Ma and Pa."

"They took Frank and maybe they took the woman I was escorting. You sure they work for Leonard Hawkins?"

"Who else? Nobody within twenty miles of this place would care one whit about Frank or me. Nobody 'cept Hawkins."

"What's his interest?"

"You know. You work for him."

"I just rode in and got lassoed into doing a chore for him. I don't know anything more than he's the town undertaker."

"He wants to gobble it all up. One by one he's stealing the ranches and farms around Espero. My pa refused to sell out at a ridiculous price, so Kenneth Hawkins foreclosed, no matter our mortgage payments were up to date."

None of this made a lick of sense to Slocum. He kept quiet, waiting for the pieces to come together so he could understand.

"Pa fought. Got himself a case of rifles and more ammunition than a whole danged Ranger company would use in a month of Sundays. No matter what Hawkins tried, Pa fought him back."

"Until?"

"Until he took them. We don't know if they're alive or dead, but Frank's sure they're dead, in spite of what Hawkins claims."

"Where would his henchmen take them—or Frank? If they swooped down, they might have taken Miss Madison, too."

"Miss Madison," mocked the woman. "She's safe enough, if they have her—and he still wants her."

"I thought tracking the gang that took Frank might lead me to both him and Miss Madison. I was wrong. I'll get on the trail back in the woods and go after whoever slugged me."

Slocum had few enough choices. Tracking Miranda in the dark would be hard, but if he had no idea where the gang, supposedly working for Hawkins, had taken Frank, he had no other choice.

"You don't know?" The woman stared at him. Her ire had finally burned itself down to an ember. Slocum saw the anger still in her, but now it went in other directions and not at him.

"Tell me. I don't even know your name."

"Polly Neville. Who're you?"

Slocum introduced himself, then asked her why she roamed around the countryside at such a late hour.

"My folks own the Box N Ranch, though how we can keep the herd intact since Hawkins has run off all our hands is a big problem."

"He kidnapped your parents? When?"

"Going on a week back's when Pa and Hawkins got into it. He makes people disappear. You never met a crueler bastard in all your born days. Pa was a fool to fight him, him with so much money and all the men you can buy. He shoulda took the pittance Hawkins offered and moved on, but he got a burr under his saddle the way he got ordered around like he was a servant."

Slocum understood how that riled a man. It was bad enough when the tax collector came around wanting to be paid, but forced to sell your ranch for a few pennies on the dollar rankled. That was outright extortion.

"He's got a gang working for him?" Slocum watched Polly as she answered and saw no trace of lying in her words.

"A dozen or more. They do what they're told because he pays them well."

"If he has so many men. why would he need me to go get his betrothed?"

"Frank said most all of Hawkins's men have been working way to the south. They ran into a cattleman who wouldn't roll over and play dead just 'cuz Hawkins said so. They've been engaged in a regular range war."

"His brother's all laid up—the town marshal. And I met the banker fellow. He was scared of his own shadow."

"That's the family," she said. "Junior Hawkins is a cold-blooded killer but can't think for himself. And Kenneth's just the same doing whatever Leonard tells him, but he's no killer."

"You think Hawkins's men took your brother?"

"Who else could it be? They already got Ma and Pa. With Frank, they have that much more leverage to make Pa sign over the Box N." She swallowed hard, then looked up at Slocum with tears in her eyes. "If threatening Ma didn't make Pa sign, nothing would. That must mean she's . . ."

"Not a bargaining chip anymore," Slocum said. He had come to the same conclusion. The elder Neville had to be kept alive to make the sale legal, but the woman was nothing more than leverage. If she died, Hawkins needed something more to hold over the rancher.

"So was your little bundle of joy carted off by Hawkins's men, too?"

"I can't see why they would bother, unless they didn't know who she was."

"As I said, the gang's been killing and raping to the south and might not recognize her." Polly rubbed her hands together. "It would be sweet revenge if they raped and killed her and

Hawkins found out." She took a deep breath, then let it out slowly. "But they're not likely to brag on it if they find out who she is. They know what Hawkins would do to them."

"She's an innocent bystander in all this. She just got in from Houston and hasn't even seen a picture of Hawkins." Slocum smiled ruefully. "She didn't even know he was an undertaker."

"Some women get hard up for a man," Polly said. "Is she real homely?"

Slocum felt the situation slipping through his fingers. Getting into a discussion with this young woman about Miranda Madison's looks did nothing to get her free of whoever stole her away nor did it free Polly's brother.

"Show me the spot where Frank was taken," he said.

"You're not with them? Cross your heart and hope to die?"

"Getting your brother back likely tells me how to find Miss Madison. She matters. Hawkins may be a scumsucking dog but he hired me to see her safely to Espero."

"Got a horse? It's a mile that way," Polly said. She stared up at the sky, catching hints of stars through the heavy clouds. "Yeah, that way."

Slocum let her fetch her own horse while he went to the barn for his. Mac's horse still stood in its stall. Whoever kidnapped Miranda had to be riding double. That tired a horse mighty fast and slowed down any retreat. He saddled and walked his horse from the barn, wondering if one stone truly killed two birds. Would finding Polly's brother also free Miranda Madison?

He mounted and trotted over to Polly. The clouds parted enough to let moonlight shine on her. He hadn't noticed how pretty she was. Miranda had a sophisticated look about her, one born of money and social standing. Polly Neville's good looks came from being out in the sun, riding the day through and enjoying it. Her auburn hair floated on the night as she trotted along. She turned and looked toward him. He couldn't tell what color those eyes were, but he guessed they were as green as his own.

"We'd better hurry. We're in for a downpour before morning," Polly warned.

"Storms come from the southeast?"

"Off the Gulf of Mexico this time of year. It's clear overhead, but back yonder's a different can of worms."

Slocum trusted her knowledge of the storm tracks. A rancher learned to feel such things in his bones. He urged his horse to a quicker gait, and less than fifteen minutes later he saw where Frank had been ambushed. It took no skill to see the man's hat in the grass—or a rifle lying nearby.

He dismounted and fetched both. Polly took the hat, but he kept the rifle. Trusting her as much as she trusted him had its drawbacks. Having a second rifle if he got into a fierce shootout meant the difference between living and dying.

Leaving his horse, he circled the area on foot. Crushed grass, trampled bushes, and a patch of cactus that had been recently kicked by horses gave him the direction. He pointed and asked, "What's that way?"

"More of Hawkins's land. Hell and damnation, most all of this is his—or will be when he steals it. The Gonzalez family had a place not a mile off. You think that's where they took Frank?"

Slocum didn't answer directly. He mounted and laid the rifle across the saddle in front of him.

"You have somewhere to hole up?"

"I'm not leaving my brother!"

"You'll get in my way."

"What if they shoot you down like a rabid dog? What if you're wounded and can't get away? I can keep after them. By all that's holy, I swear I *will* get them."

Slocum knew his choices were few. He could hog-tie Polly and leave her here, but if her dire prediction came true and he was killed, she might die if she couldn't get free. If he tied her so poorly she could get free eventually, she'd be on his trail in a flash. Taking her horse would only slow her down.

"Stay back a few yards. Keep that rifle of yours in its sheath. I don't want you accidentally shooting me in the back."

"It won't be by accident if you're lying to me."

Slocum had to laugh. She had sand.

"Why are you laughing?"

"Be quiet," Slocum said. He took a deep whiff of the night air. Mingled with the earth and vegetation came a hint of the rain Polly had predicted. He also caught wood smoke. Turning like a weather vane, he found the direction and listened hard. The distant sound of horses told him how close he was to finding at least a few riders.

He motioned for her to follow. She had the good sense to obey him and hung back until he found a dirt road. Then she came up beside him.

"The Gonzalez house is just around the bend in the road."

"Where's the road go?" He looked behind them. The dirt tracks disappeared into a stand of trees.

"On to the main road, then into Espero."

"A day's travel?"

"More or less," she said. "This is a good place for Hawkins to keep the people he wants to torture." Polly's voice rose when she said, "Might be my folks are here, too. All three of them, Frank and my parents."

Slocum hefted the rifle, checked to be sure a round rested in the chamber, then rode slowly forward. At the bend in the road, he brought the rifle to his shoulder, but no target centered on his sights.

"The fire's too high to have burned longer than a few minutes," Slocum said. "Wait for my signal, then come on in." He glanced at Polly's rifle. The unspoken order made her draw the weapon and clutch it fiercely.

He dropped to the ground and advanced on the house. The slight breeze made the house creak. Other than the scurrying of small forest animals, he heard nothing. A quick look in one window showed the kitchen where the fire had been built in an iron stove. Slocum ducked back, edged around to the door, then kicked it in. If anything had moved, he would have fired.

Empty.

A quick search of the house further disappointed him. Here and there he saw traces of men being present recently. Whatever had brought them here took them away as quickly. He left the house and headed for the barn when he heard Polly shriek.

He reversed his course and ran back to find her on hands and knees, digging like a prairie dog. In the pale moonlight he traced out the rectangular pattern of a freshly dug grave.

"He's here," she sobbed. "Frank's here. Help me dig him up. Help me. Please!"

Knowing what he would find, Slocum lent a hand. But a few minutes of digging revealed something he never expected to see—ever.

5

The pinewood coffin lid had cracked and fingers poked through. Slocum worked alongside Polly to get more dirt away from the lid so he could wrap his own fingers around the lid and yank hard. Dust flew everywhere as the lid broke into three pieces. Slocum tumbled back and sat in the dirt, staring as Frank Neville sat up in the coffin and spat dirt from his mouth.

"H-He tried to do it to me," he gasped out. He stared directly at Slocum with nothing but pure terror in his eyes.

"Those men—Hawkins's gang—they buried you alive?" Slocum got to his knees and edged closer.

Staring into the coffin told him that was exactly what had happened. Huge curls of wood had been gouged from the sides of the coffin where Neville fought to get free. In some places it looked as if a router rather than fingernails had been used to form the deep trenches in the wood. But the man's bloody, broken fingernails told the story.

"I had to get out. Didn't know how deep they'd planted me, but I hoped they were lazy bastards." Neville turned to one side and puked, wiped his mouth, and then got to his feet.

He let Polly help him but shied away from Slocum.

"He's one of 'em," he accused. "I shot McIntyre. Couldn't get a decent bead on this one."

"Where's the woman who was with me? Did Hawkins's men have her?" Slocum grabbed a double handful of the man's coat and shook him like a terrier would a rat. Neville's head snapped back and forth as strength fled from his body.

"Stop it! Can't you see what he's been through? He would have died here if I hadn't found him in time." Polly pushed Slocum away and clung to her weak brother. Getting her legs under her body and arms wrapped around him, she heaved Neville to his feet so he could step out of the coffin.

"He helped, Frank, he really did. Hawkins had duped him. He's not one of the gang."

"Doin' what Hawkins wants is same as bein' one of the gang."

Slocum let the pair of them make their way to the house while he prowled about. He had no trouble finding the tracks of several horses, perhaps a half dozen, riding toward the road that Polly said went to Espero. The gang returned to report to their boss. He sat heavily on a stump used as a chopping block and wiped away the dirt from his coat and then rubbed his hands as clean as he could.

Hearing only one side of what had to be a deadly feud prejudiced him against Hawkins, but the undertaker might have good explanations for what was going on. He might not have kidnapped the elder Nevilles. In spite of what Polly thought, they might have taken the money and left the region without telling their children. Slocum leaned forward and put his head on his hands. That made no sense. Unless Hawkins had paid them and demanded they leave without telling their children, but why do that?

His head threatened to explode. When a sudden flash almost blinded him, he thought his head had blown apart. Heavy raindrops spatted against the brim of his hat. As he turned his face to the sky, several cold drops hit him in the eyes. His headache deepened as his eyes became swelled grapes pulsing against his eyelids.

He swung about and headed for the house. Its roof looked intact. Even if it wasn't, there had to be a dry spot where he could recover his senses and figure out what to do next. Hiring on to chaperon Miranda Madison wore heaviest on him. The bump on the top of his head gave a constant reminder of failing at that job. He had taken money, even if only a few dollars remained of the first payment. To collect the four hundred dollars remaining of the agreed-upon fee, he had to deliver Miss Madison into Hawkins's hands. The only problem with that was not knowing where she was.

New pain lanced into his head, and he explored the bloody bump he had acquired hunting for her. The sounds he had heard earlier were likely Polly and her brother. Maybe the Hawkins gang shooting at them. Had Miranda beaned him? Why? They were getting along just fine, and she showed no hesitation about Espero or meeting her husband-to-be. If anything, she accepted her new role as wife with great enthusiasm. Greater enthusiasm than Slocum would have expected, at any rate, but he had met Hawkins and she had yet to have that pleasure.

He pushed hard against the door into the kitchen. It resisted. He pushed harder. It suddenly gave way, sending him facedown onto the floor. Not an inch from his nose was a pair of scuffed boots. Arching his back, he looked up into a rifle held in rock-steady hands. Sighting down the barrel, Frank Neville had him dead to rights.

"Either pull the trigger and put me out of my misery or help me up."

Slocum saw that Neville intended to shoot him. With a combination of wiggle and dive, he got his arms around the man's knees and drove his shoulder into his right shin. The rifle discharged, but the bullet went high, breaking out a pane of glass that had somehow survived to this point.

Knowing better than to let up, Slocum swarmed up the man's body. The smell of dirt—earth from a grave—clung to Neville like a poisonous perfume. Slocum clawed his way up and slammed his shoulder against the rifle barrel as Neville fired again. The burning sensation on his arm came from the heated barrel, not from a bullet. With the smell of dirt and gun smoke in his nostrils, Slocum grabbed hard on Neville's shirt and slammed him backward. His head banged against a chair. This gave Slocum time to yank the rifle from his hand and use it to bludgeon his attacker.

"Stop! What are you doing? Stop!"

Polly's cry kept Slocum from ramming the rifle stock into her brother's face. He used the rifle as a crutch to stand. She stared at him, aghast.

"Why'd you hit him? Frank didn't do anything!"

"Kill you, you miserable . . ." Neville's words trickled away.

Polly cradled him in her arms. Whatever he whispered to her caused the woman to drop him. His head hit the floor with a loud thud.

"You're so stupid, flies wouldn't land on you, Franklin Pierce Neville! He helped me. You had no call trying to gun him down again."

Slocum nudged her, pressing the rifle into her hands. She stared at the weapon then up at Slocum. Her mouth thinned to a razor slash, and she launched into berating her brother some more.

Slocum left them in the kitchen and found a dry patch in the front room to sit. The storm gathered fury, but the roof held. Only when the wind blew rain parallel to the ground did the walls start leaking. Slocum ignored the small spray coming after him and closed his eyes. The lump on the top of his head throbbed now and sent dull waves of pain through his head and neck. Other cuts and scrapes on his body and arms hardly bothered him, or at least not as much as worry over Miranda Madison's fate.

"You have to excuse my brother. He's been through hell."

"Getting buried alive can do that," Slocum said.

"It's how Hawkins punishes everyone. Who's not afraid of being treated that way? Frank was lucky we were so close."

"You learned one thing," Slocum said, closing his eyes and stretching out on the floor. "He wasn't kidnapped to be used to force your pa to sign over the ranch. Otherwise, he would have been buried in front of him. Just telling your pa that Frank was buried would only steel his resolve. He'd think they were lying to him."

"You're mighty smart, John Slocum." She put her hand on his chest lightly, teasingly. "How'd that come about?"

"Been dropped on my head one too many times," Slocum said. He took off his hat to show her where he had been struck.

"That lump's the size of the Alamo! Don't flinch."

She tore off part of her already disheveled blouse and soaked it in rainwater puddling nearby. With surprisingly tender touches, she dabbed away the caked blood. As she bent over him, her chest was only inches from his face. Slocum couldn't help noticing the gentle sway of her breasts as she moved or how the rips and tears exposed deliciously naked titflesh.

Polly stopped and looked down at him, her breasts just inches from his face.

"Do you need a written invite?" She shimmied a little, causing quakes in her breasts. By pulling back her shoulders, she contrived to get one teat entirely free. Naked and inviting, she lowered her chest so that a dark brown nipple brushed his lips.

"Your brother's ready to kill me, just because," Slocum said.

"Frank's passed out in the kitchen. Are you passed out here? When you can have this?"

Her breast moved a fraction of an inch lower. Slocum's

resolve vanished. His tongue flicked out and rolled around the hard nub of flesh. Polly moaned softly, the sound lost in the crash of rain against the walls and roof. When a dazzling flash of lightning lit the room, Slocum got the best view yet of her. Her eyes were closed and she chewed on her lower lip. Auburn hair turned to mahogany as the afterimage from the flash faded, but the nearness of her warm flesh remained.

Slocum sucked the entire tit into his mouth. Using his tongue, he rolled around the blood-engorged pebble at the summit, then tried to mash it down into the soft flesh beneath. Polly sank lower, shoving her chest out in such a way to force even more into his mouth. He obliged. Using his teeth to lightly score the soft slopes, he worked back until only the cherry-sized bud remained between his lips. Then he used teeth and lips and sucked for all he was worth. Polly arched her back and tried to jam herself into his mouth fully.

He wasn't having any of that. He wanted to arouse her—and he did when he used his tongue to slither about in the canyon between her tits. She shuddered as he worked his way from one snowy crest to the other, taking plenty of time to lave the nips and suckle on them until he felt as if he would explode.

"I want more, John," she said, her lips touching his ear. She nibbled at his earlobe.

"Got to get free of these jeans."

He almost erupted like a young buck when she reached down and pressed hard into the bulge at his crotch. Her fingers danced about and magically freed his fly one button at a time. He snapped to attention like a soldier on parade. Her fingers curled about him and began stroking up and down until he was steelier than he ever had been. Keeping himself under control proved hard when she began tapping her fingertips lightly on his balls. Everything tumbled and churned inside him.

Slocum arched his back and moved her around so they lay side by side. She started to protest, but he cut her off with a deep kiss. Her lips parted slightly, allowing him to invade. His tongue flashed out and teased her tongue before engaging in an erotic hide-and-seek that took away both their breaths.

They rolled over, Polly's legs parting.

"I don't have anything on underneath," she said in a sex-husky voice.

His exploring hand found she told the truth. He pushed up her riding skirt and found warm inner thigh. He stroked over it. Every touch on the sleek skin sent ripples of desire throughout her body. He knew that from the way she moaned and curled up, her knees rising so she could wantonly open herself for him.

He ached from need, but he wanted her to feel the same anticipation. His finger invaded her core, wiggled about in the damp heat, and then slipped back out. Dampened fingers slathered her own inner oils all over the pinkly scalloped nether lips. When he found the tiny spire at the top of her sex lips, he squeezed down just a little.

Polly let out a shriek that would wake the dead. He retreated for a moment, but her hand found his beneath her skirts and held it in place.

"Don't you dare leave, not now," she said.

"Frank—"

"Is out like a light. And if he comes in, to hell with him!" She passionately kissed Slocum until his lips bruised.

He hardly noticed. His hands were too busy exploring the mysteries of her body, finding places to touch and arouse and bring gasps of delight to her lips. He kissed over her eyes, to her ear, and then worked down her neck and finally to the valley where he had begun.

"Now, John, now!"

She wasn't to be denied. Neither was he. Slocum moved

between her legs, ran his arms under her knees, and lifted, bending her almost double. In this position he bent forward, hips thrusting. The plum-colored tip of his manhood brushed across her most intimate flesh, then parted the curtains and sank balls deep within. They both cried out at the smooth, quick insertion.

She felt tight and hot and wet all around him. He looked down into her half-opened eyes and saw the lust boiling there. It fed his own. He pulled back slightly, letting her legs relax a mite. Then he rushed back in, again bending her double. With the rain pounding outside, they continued their lovemaking until neither could stand another instant. Slocum felt her tense and clutch at his buried length. This triggered his own eruption. He spilled into her needy, greedy interior as he continued stroking.

When he was drained and his organ limp, he sank down atop her to give her a slow, tender kiss.

"Never felt like that before, during, or after," Polly said in a tiny voice. She stared at him, and he saw a touch of fear.

"You don't have to be afraid of anything."

"With you here," she said. He didn't know exactly what she meant but everything crashed in on him now.

His head no longer throbbed but exhaustion from the day—and Polly—consumed him like a hungry animal with its prey. He held her in his arms and felt her soft breath against his neck. The rain hid the world, and all he needed was right here, in his arms.

He awoke in the morning with bright sunlight slanting through a broken window. Slocum flopped onto his back, laced his fingers under his head, and stared up at the ceiling, where water stains on the plaster betrayed spots leaking in the roof. He listened to the animals moving about outside in the fresh, clean dawn.

And he heard nothing in the house except for creaking sounds as it settled on its foundations. Without poking around, he knew Polly and her brother were both gone. He sat up, buttoned his fly, and got to his feet. It was time he was on the trail, too.

He had to find Miranda Madison, no matter how unimportant that had seemed only a few hours earlier.

6

Slocum took his sweet time moving around, being certain his feet worked fine and his head didn't cause dizziness when he least expected it. He attributed his recovery from the aches and pains of the day before to his lovemaking with Polly Neville. That she and her brother had left before he awoke didn't surprise him. Polly would find it uncomfortable if her brother started bad-mouthing him as being one of Hawkins's thugs.

He found his pinto, did what he could to clean off the saddle, and then made sure grass and water were adequate as a way of apologizing. He usually cared for his horses better than he had the night before. The rain and . . . events . . . had made him careless. Once in the saddle, he rode slowly, trying to find tracks along the road.

The rain had erased all trace of Hawkins's gang. He cut through the woods and found the abandoned house where he had intended to spend the night with Miranda Madison. The least he could do was tend Mac's horse, hitch it up, and drive into Espero to let Hawkins know what had happened. Good sense told him to ride north as fast as he could go, but he had taken the undertaker's money to escort Miranda safely to Espero, and he had failed. How he would break the news mattered. He might have to shoot his way out of town, though he wanted to avoid that.

Most of all, he didn't want to be sent back out to find Miranda. Finding her after the heavy rains would be a matter of luck rather than skill, unless Hawkins had overheard some town gossip.

He rode up to the house, then slowed and finally halted entirely. Something had changed from the night before when he had left Miranda fixing supper inside the house and he had been slugged in the woods. Slocum studied the house for a full minute before it hit him what was wrong.

"The buggy's gone," he said softly. He received a neigh from his horse, chiding him for not seeing this right away.

A quick check in the barn showed Mac's horse was missing, too. The rain had removed any spoor to read, but the lack of hoofprints and buggy wheel imprints in the ground told him someone had hitched up the horse and ridden off before or during the storm.

Inside, the supper Miranda had fixed had become fodder for more bugs than he could count.

"At least the rest of the food didn't go to waste." He hoisted the burlap bag with the remainder of their victuals. His belly growled.

Slocum took the time to fix some bacon, biscuits, and peaches from an airtight. He washed it all down with coffee he had boiled over a new fire. While he might catch up with the buggy sooner, the half hour he took to eat mattered less than the satisfaction of a full belly. Finding the buggy would be a matter of luck more than skill.

He packed what supplies were left, slung them over the rump of his horse, and set out to find Miranda. At the road he considered riding back toward Dexter Junction, buying himself a ticket on the next train out, and simply getting the hell away from Espero. He had a fifty-fifty chance of over-taking the buggy.

Instead, he turned his horse's face toward Espero and trotted along. The clean, clear air filled his lungs and revived him as much as the food. The rolling hills and thick vegetation proved peaceful and allowed him to settle down enough to think about breaking the news to Leonard Hawkins that his mail-order bride had been spirited off in the night. The worst Slocum could imagine was Hawkins demanding his money back. Slocum might have to work off the money he had spent for the buggy and supplies, but that would be it.

He touched the butt of his six-shooter. He wouldn't accept any punishment, not from Leonard Hawkins, not from men riding for him who buried men alive for the pure cussedness of the act. The worst he would take off Hawkins was non-payment of the rest of the promised money. Even then, Slocum considered asking for reimbursement for the buggy.

The woods opened into a level plain of high grass and occasional trees, giving him a clear view almost a mile along the road. He drew rein, fished for his field glasses in his saddlebags, and carefully adjusted them on a tiny dot on the road ahead.

"I'll be damned," he muttered.

Slocum replaced the field glasses and put his heels to his horse. He kept the gait under a gallop, not wanting to wear out the animal. By the time he reached the spot where he had seen the buggy, the driver had disappeared along another forested section of road. Advancing slower now, he overtook the buggy at the outskirts of Espero.

From behind he couldn't see the driver, but the destination was obvious. The driver went to Espero.

"Stop!" Slocum's voice carried. To his surprise, the driver obeyed right away.

He rode up beside the buggy. Holding down his anger, Slocum tipped his hat to Miranda Madison.

"Pleased to see you're not dead," he said. "Where did you go last night?"

"I can ask the same!" The woman gripped the reins so hard her hands shook. "You left me back there!"

"Somebody slugged me. When I came to, you were gone. The buggy was there, but you were gone."

"I was not," Miranda said, but her denial carried no conviction. "Where would I have gone?"

"I went hunting for you and ran into a gang that buries its victims alive."

"What?"

"I thought that might have happened to you. I went back to the house but the buggy was gone."

"Of course it was. You abandoned me, so I pressed on by myself."

Slocum tried to figure out when she had left to reach town by now. The only thing he could come up with was her leaving in the middle of the downpour. That made no sense, but it had to be so. The horse couldn't pull the buggy fast enough for her to have started after the storm died down.

"You didn't see anyone prowling around the house after I left?"

"You went out for firewood and never came back. That's all I know. And to answer your question, sir, I saw no one."

Slocum started to tell her she was a good liar, but a liar nonetheless.

"Are you on your way to Hawkins's funeral parlor?"

"I don't know where it is, but someone in town must be able to direct me."

Slocum trotted off, not caring if she followed. He turned down a street crossing Main and glanced over his shoulder. Miranda guided the buggy after him. Slocum dismounted in front of Hawkins's business, not sure what he would say when he faced the undertaker.

"This is his place of business?" Miranda looked skeptical. "You did say Mr. Hawkins was a mortician."

Slocum held out his hand to help her from the buggy. She ignored him and got out on her own. She tilted her nose up, brushed mud from her dress, and stalked off to meet her betrothed.

As Slocum followed, he looked back along the street. A mounted man quickly wheeled about and galloped off. He wore a yellow slicker mostly torn away on the right side. Slocum caught a glimpse of the man's iron slung low on his hip. A gunman.

"Are you joining me, Mr. Slocum?" Miranda tried to sound impatient. Her voice almost cracked with strain. Meeting Leonard Hawkins was something she was loath to do alone.

Slocum didn't blame her because he knew what was ahead. But she could only be apprehensive about meeting her groom-to-be because it was the first time she would lay eyes on him.

"Just taking in the sights," he said. He gave her a once-over. "You want to check into a hotel and freshen up?"

"I am anxious." Her eyes darted to the single case in the buggy. She couldn't have stuffed a great deal of additional clothing in such a small valise. What she wore might be her finest clothing since she had expected to meet Hawkins at Dexter Junction and hadn't changed since leaving the train.

He held the door, and she brushed past. Miranda was a lovely woman, prettier than Polly Neville, but where Polly was open about her feelings—in all things, as Slocum could attest—this woman held everything in. She never quite told the truth and always hid feelings, trying to be the proper lady. How that would play out when she was married to the man in town dealing exclusively with dead bodies wasn't anything Slocum wanted to see.

The funeral parlor's interior was dim, and a hint of perfume made Slocum's nose wrinkle. Miranda sneezed. The coffins on either side of the vestibule formed a gauntlet leading to the curtained back room. Slocum pointed ahead.

Miranda swallowed hard, settled her shoulders, and walked gallantly forward, head high. Slocum trailed, but he stopped dead in his tracks when he saw Hawkins in the curtained room with the bier.

The man stood on the dais polishing a fancy wood casket. He stroked back and forth with his soft rag, leaving a trail of shining wood behind as he worked.

"I will be with you in a moment."

He sounded breathless from his task. Slocum didn't see any sweat beading the portly man's forehead. That made him wonder at the excitement Hawkins seemed to take from working on the coffin.

"Are you Mr. Hawkins? I am Miranda Madison."

"Yes, yes, a moment," Hawkins said, rubbing a small section of the polished wood with his elbow to get off the last trace of polish. He stood and faced her, smiling. "Your entrance to Espero was relayed to me immediately. I knew it had to be you, my dear."

"Not a whole lot of other women coming to town," Slocum said. "No one else accompanied by me either."

Hawkins cast a quick look at the casket, then gingerly slid his fingers under the lid and lifted. Pale blue satin lined the box. Hawkins ran his fingers over the interior and looked as if he got a sexual thrill out of it.

"Would you like to lie in it, Miss Madison?"

"I beg your pardon!" She recoiled and stepped back, bumping into Slocum.

"As one of my wedding presents, I will construct the finest casket anyone has ever seen. I'll form the interior to your voluptuous figure. As to your clothing when you are in repose—"

"I am *not* dead, sir!"

"No, of course not, but one day you shall be. We all will. Preparing for that melancholy moment is what keeps me alive, in business."

Slocum saw how Miranda started to turn and leave. Any

normal woman would have, hearing how her betrothed already considered her dead and laid to rest in a coffin. She checked her movement, rubbed her palms against her skirts, and stepped forward.

"You do fine work, sir."

"Please, call me Leonard."

"Your craftsmanship is superb, Leonard."

"I know." He rubbed over the liner again, then reached out and touched her cheek.

From where Slocum stood, he saw the rippling in the hair at the back of her neck as she forced herself to keep from recoiling. Miranda had her reasons for wanting to marry Hawkins. What they might be when a woman as articulate and beautiful could have any man eluded Slocum.

"You are so skilled and successful," she said, stepping onto the dais. She reached for Hawkins's arm, then veered away to run her fingers over the satin. "Such elegance."

"Yes, yes, my dear. We are going to be so happy together."

"Can I get my pay?" Slocum called. Miranda jumped. Hawkins glared at him. "I can be on my way as soon as you give me the four hundred you owe."

"Four hundred? Yes, that was what I said." Hawkins frowned. "However, you allowed Mr. McIntyre to be gunned down. Where is his body?"

"I buried it."

If Slocum had rammed a hot branding iron up Hawkins's fat ass, he couldn't have gotten a bigger reaction. Fury turned his face red, and he clenched his hands into shaking fists.

"You buried him yourself? You had the gall to bury him?"

"Along the road to Dexter Junction," Slocum said, egging the man on and not knowing why.

His smartest course of action was to keep quiet, get paid, and leave Espero as fast as his horse could gallop. Instead, he couldn't stop goading the undertaker.

"I was going to say words over the grave, but I didn't

know what Mac would have wanted." Slocum saw this jibe had less effect than telling Hawkins he had buried him. "I couldn't find his horse to take the blanket, so I just put him in the dirt not far from where he was cut down. You want me to tell the marshal about it so he can track down the killer?"

Hawkins sputtered. Burying his henchman without so much as a blanket had lit his fuse again.

"Please, Leonard, pay Mr. Slocum so we can be alone. So we can become better . . . acquainted." Miranda brushed her dark hair away from her eyes. They were twin beacons of anger directed at Slocum for riling up her betrothed. She laid her hand on the undertaker's arm. He shook her off.

"Very well. It is for the best that Mr. Slocum be gone."

"You want to retrieve the body so you can bury it in the town's potter's field?" Slocum kept nettling the man because he had taken a real dislike to him. "I can show Junior where to dig."

"Take your blood money," Hawkins said. He pulled out a roll of greenbacks large enough to choke a cow. He peeled off the bills, then tossed them in Slocum's direction.

The money fluttered in the air and slowly fell to the carpeted floor. Slocum stood stock-still, waiting for the bills to land before he bent over and picked them up one by one. He made a big show of counting then before he tucked them into his coat pocket, as if he didn't trust Hawkins to give him the proper amount. Then he looked up.

"You owe me for the buggy I bought for her."

"Get out!" Hawkins turned red in the face.

Slocum thought the man would attack him. He would have welcomed that to give himself a safety valve for blowing off steam after getting shot at nurse-maiding Miranda back to Espero. Something about the set to his shoulders warned Hawkins to back off. The man fished out three twenty-dollar bills. Before he could drop them, Slocum snatched the money from his hand.

"Thanks. We're square." Slocum touched the brim of his hat in Miranda's direction.

Her face had frozen into an emotionless mask.

Slocum started to make a parting comment, then common sense finally took over. He stuffed the money for the buggy purchase into his pocket with the rest of the money and pushed through the heavy velvet drapes. All sound from the inner viewing room was muffled, but he knew Miranda was telling Hawkins how glad she was to have come. What the undertaker said back to her wasn't sweet nothings. Slocum smiled wryly, thinking how the man detailed for her how he wanted to make a custom casket as a wedding present.

He wasn't sure she deserved such a husband, but she had made her own bed. It was time for her to lie in it.

He stepped out into the humid afternoon and sucked in a deep breath. Freedom. He was free of his enforced employment, and it was time to ride on. Slocum swung up into the saddle and turned back toward Espero's main street. The lure of a shot of whiskey to celebrate proved easy enough to overcome as he thought of putting as much distance between him and the undertaker as possible.

Hawkins hadn't relinquished the money easily. Had this been a show for his new bride? Miranda had certainly licked her lips when she saw the roll of bills the undertaker had pulled from his pocket. Not many men went around with such a poke. Nothing in the way Hawkins had handled the money hinted that this was an unusual amount to carry.

"I hope you both get what you want," Slocum said softly as he rode west. "Whatever that is."

With the setting sun in his face, he decided to camp for the night a couple miles outside town. Adding more miles to his back trail appealed to him, but he had been through too much in the past few days and wanted a rest.

As he pitched camp and prepared a fire, he poked at the coals and thought of the night spent with Polly. That had been the best thing that had happened to him since first riding into Espero, and that included the five hundred dollars Hawkins had paid. The fragrant smoke from a dried post oak limb he fed into the fire made his belly rumble in memory of food cooked over such fires before. He worked to prepare a decent meal. When daylight broke the next morning, he intended to be on the trail. Something made him uneasy about Espero and the way Hawkins acted.

The man might be a lunatic, but he was a rich and powerful one. All that made for a dangerous mix Slocum was inclined to avoid.

After finishing his supper, cleaning the tin plate, and dashing the last of the coffee into the fire to drench the embers, he lay back, head on his saddle and staring up at the stars. The prior night's storm had fled, leaving a perfect sky. He pulled up the blanket around his shoulders and rolled over.

As he drifted to sleep, movement pulled him back to the world around him. He gripped his six-shooter, rolled over, cocked, and fired. The man behind him let out a yelp of pain and staggered back.

Then a loud *whish*!

Slocum tried to avoid the club that smashed into his head. He failed. His six-gun fell from numbed fingers. Then the club crashed down again on his head and everything went away.

7

Slocum coughed, tried to get his breath, and then screamed as he thrashed about, hands crashing into the wood sides of a coffin. He shook his head to get sweat from his eyes, but open or closed, free of sweat or not, those eyes were met only with complete darkness.

He tried to suck in another breath. The air was turning bad. A stint working as a miner in a deep gold mine had inured him to darkness, heat, and lack of air, but there had been a way to move about in the mine, even if he wiggled along a stope flat on his belly while tons of rock pressed into his back. He kicked and found only wood. Pushing upward, his head rubbed against rough pinewood. A lump on his left side made him roll slightly to his right so he could reach his cross-draw holster.

Whoever had buried him had left him his pistol.

Wild thoughts jumbled and confused him. He was buried six feet under, doomed to suffocate in the cramped dark coffin. Suicide. Take the six-shooter out and shoot himself. End it now. No escape.

Slocum roared in rage. The next time he fired his Colt,

it would be aimed at the head of the man who had buried him alive.

Recovering, he forced himself to breathe slowly and shallowly. Slocum began exploring his wooden prison. Kicking loosened the end panel of the coffin. Pushing hard caused nails to creak above his head, but he got no traction in forcing away the side panels. He lifted his knees and tried to push up the lid. Small cascades of dirt tumbled around the edges when he forced up a fraction of an inch. He collapsed, gasping for breath. He was close to death, and there was nothing he could do to escape.

He gripped the butt of his six-gun again and got even madder at whoever had done this to him. The gang working for Hawkins had buried Frank Neville this way. Whether Leonard Hawkins had ordered them to put Slocum underground didn't matter. If they worked for the undertaker, they would die. So would Hawkins.

He futilely kicked again and only caused some dust to float up to his nose, making him sneeze. He sank back, all strength gone. Closing his eyes, he worked through other possible ways of escaping. Thoughts blurring and harder to follow as he ran out of air, he realized he was starting to hallucinate. Voices mocked him. The scrape of metal on the coffin lid promised salvation, but he knew that wasn't possible.

Then he gasped as fresh air rushed into his face. He opened his eyes and got dirt in them, but this didn't stop him from lifting his six-shooter, ready to fling lead in all directions.

"Settle down, John, you're not dead. Not yet."

"Polly?"

Strong hands grabbed his arms and lifted him up. He tried to take a step and fell forward on the edge of the opened grave.

"How'd you find me?" He swung around and sat on the edge of the grave. He had been buried three feet under. Slocum wasn't sure if that irritated him. His would-be killers hadn't bothered to bury him properly. At that depth, scavengers would have dug him up in a week or two when he started decomposing and the smell drew them to an easy meal.

He bushed dirt off his face and peered up at Polly. Beside her, leaning on a shovel, Frank Neville glared at him.

"We're even," Neville said. He hoisted the shovel to his shoulder and stalked off.

"Hell of a way to get even," Slocum said. He got to his feet. "How *did* you come to dig me up?"

"Frank and I tried to grab one of Hawkins's gang to make him talk."

"To find your ma and pa?"

Polly nodded. She began pacing about, not looking at him as if she felt guilty.

"I saw you with the whore Hawkins bought. I wanted to nab the son of a bitch named Julian who seems to be the leader of the gang working for Hawkins, but you came out 'fore I spotted him. You rode off."

"And Julian followed me out of town," Slocum said. "I should have paid more attention to my back trail."

"Yeah, you should have. Julian and four others lit out after you with a cheap coffin tied down to a pack horse. There was nothing Frank or I could do against five of them. We overtook them as they were finishing with the last spade of dirt on your grave."

Slocum patted his pockets. The money Hawkins had paid him was gone. This was another score he had to settle. Men tried to kill him all too often, but doing it to steal back money turned the motives from personal to venal. That defined the undertaker more than anything else in his mind.

"Where did they go? This Julian and the men riding with him?"

Polly shrugged. The movement caught his attention. She noticed his interest in the way her blouse moved about and smiled wryly.

"I see you aren't entirely dead."

"Parts of me are more alive than others."

"Might be those parts can get another workout," she said, staring boldly at him.

"After we get your ma and pa back," he said.

"You're not only horny, you're smart," she said. "I'm not sure if that's a compliment."

"I'll take it as such," Slocum said, stretching.

He then checked his Colt Navy to be sure the dirt hadn't fouled the mechanism. The pistol never failed him because he tended it carefully. Too many men let their six-shooters rust in their holsters. For them, it would have been better going unarmed since they wouldn't have the false security of a six-gun coming into their grips and firing dead on target.

"You two going to spend the rest of eternity lollygagging or are we going to get on the trail?"

"Your brother's anxious to die," Slocum said.

"He's like me. Anxious to put those snakes into a grave where they belong."

Slocum had to admit he shared this with Polly and her brother.

"They didn't even bother taking your horse," Polly said. "Or it ran off and they weren't inclined to chase after it."

Slocum patted his empty vest pocket again. Julian and his partners had been in a hurry, but not enough of one that they didn't search him.

"You have any plan to find your parents, other than kidnapping Julian?"

"You make it sound like that's not going to work." Polly glared at him. "I'm beginning to think we made a mistake bothering to dig you back up."

"Hawkins is the man you want, not his lackeys."

"That's easy to say, John, but he has bodyguards around him all the time. They're not always easy to spot. When they aren't there, his brother is."

"Junior?" Slocum pursed his lips. "The marshal looks like a weak link in the Hawkins family."

"How do you intend to break that chain?"

Slocum thought hard, then looked up.

"Your brother's gone. He rode a ways, then galloped like there was no tomorrow."

"Frank!" Polly ran ahead of Slocum and looked down the road in the direction of Espero. "Oh, no, Frank, you crazy—"

"Let's ride," Slocum said. He swung up and felt his horse shudder under him, getting used to his weight once more. "You figure he's going straight for Hawkins?"

"Where else? You were right about the cause of all the trouble in these parts. Hawkins wants to own it all. Get rid of him and the problems go away."

"Kill him and you might never find your ma and pa," Slocum said. He snapped his reins and got his horse into a long lope.

Slocum didn't bother sharing his opinion that Polly and Frank's parents were already dead. Hawkins pretended to keep things legal, demanding the elder Neville's signature to make the land transfer legal, but with both the marshal and the bank president his brothers, all Hawkins had to do was forge the signature. Who would contest it? Hawkins had some twisted sense a forced signature on a bill of sale was legal and a forged one wasn't, but the result was the same.

Twilight sank down around him, dulling details and bringing out the bugs. Slocum pulled up his bandanna to keep them out of his nose and mouth. The buzzing around his ears almost drowned out the thunder of his horse's hooves and the occasional curse Polly threw at her brother, Hawkins, and the world in general. At least she didn't seem to include Slocum in the things that had gone wrong in Espero.

He was so lost in the ride and planning what to do once

they overtook Frank that he failed to see movement on either side of the road ahead until it was too late. Coming from the shadowy thickets came four riders, two on either side.

The air filled with bullets that rivaled the bugs with their nasty whines. He jerked to one side when a hot streak ran across the top of his shoulder. The sudden shift caused his horse to stumble, spilling Slocum to the ground. He landed on his right side, arm pinned beneath him as he skidded along.

Behind him came the sharp crack of a rifle. This produced immediate confusion among the four men attacking him.

"He's got a partner. Kill him!"

That order was the last the outlaw gave. A rifle bullet struck him smack in the middle of the chest. He threw up his hands, twisted slightly, and then joined Slocum on the ground. The three remaining road agents' horses reared and sent their shots wildly into the owl-light, giving Slocum the chance to get to his knees. He shook his right arm to get feeling back, then drew and fired in a smooth movement.

His bullet missed, but the stir caused proved more useful than if he had dropped one of the remaining riders. The outlaws' horses bucked even harder. Slocum ran forward, not shooting, waiting for a decent target. When he came close enough to worry about how the rearing horse would lash out at him with his front hooves, he aimed and fired. The rider grunted and bent double but did not fall off the horse. Slocum shot again and missed. The man's horse spun around and tried to kick Slocum with its rear hooves.

Polly came to a halt beside him, the still-smoking rifle in her hands.

"They're getting away. Get your horse. We have to stop them."

"They were only road agents," Slocum said. Then he looked up at her. The darkness hid her face, but the set to her body told the story. "Those were Julian's gang?"

"I take back what I said about you being smart. Of course they were."

Slocum checked the dead outlaw on the ground, hands patting him down in search of any of the money that had been taken from him. The outlaw's pockets were as empty as Slocum's. He spun and caught the reins thrown in his direction. Polly had run down his horse and brought it back.

"Three of them left," she said grimly. "I winged one."

"I gut-shot another."

That explained why they had run away, though they outnumbered Slocum and Polly. Two of them were wounded, one seriously.

"Was Julian with them? I couldn't tell. I was too far away."

Slocum admitted he had never seen Julian and asked what he looked like.

"Real thin face, like a hatchet. Got a burn scar on his left cheek. Ugly son of a bitch. His eyes are the worst. All deadlike and blacker than the ace of spades. They bore right into your soul."

Slocum slowed his headlong pace and straightened to get a better look at the road ahead. A bend in the road gave a perfect spot for an ambush, and he told Polly as much. She showed good sense by slowing and finally pulling up beside him.

"What are we going to do?" she asked. "We can't be fraidy-cats, or we'll never catch them."

"We don't know who they are," Slocum said. "None of them was Julian, or did you see him?"

Polly shook her head and started to speak, then clamped her mouth shut as she realized what Slocum was saying.

"We need to get after your brother. He's going to get himself in a world of trouble." Slocum worried that the road agents were part of Julian's gang—part of *Hawkins's* gang—and had let Frank ride past into worse trouble.

"Hawkins enjoys playing with people like a cat plays with a mouse," she said.

"All the more reason to forget the road agents and find Frank."

Polly reluctantly rode on, then tapped her heels against her horse's flanks to pick up the gait. Slocum followed now, wary of the darkness along the sides of the road. Any hint of movement made him jump needlessly until he settled down. The injuries the men had taken likely sent them to a doctor, not into a new ambush. None of the men he had seen matched Julian's description. If they ever were his gang, he might have ridden back to Espero to let Hawkins know Slocum had been taken care of.

He touched his empty vest pocket for the hundredth time and got mad all over again. Burying him alive was one thing; stealing his money was another. Either dictated that he put a slug into the heart of the coward who was responsible.

"There's the edge of town," Polly said after they had ridden for a considerable spell. Slocum had lost track of time but noticed his horse was beginning to falter.

"What would Frank do? Go straight to Hawkins's funeral parlor?"

"He had built up such a head of steam, he's likely to buy dynamite and blow the place up."

Slocum doubted that. Anger such as Frank's required personal vindication. Frank wanted to sight down the gun barrel as he shot Hawkins. If Neville even thought about it and held his anger in check, he had to pry the information about his parents from Hawkins. The undertaker would say anything to stay alive and wait for Julian and the rest of his gang to show up.

"He'll take Hawkins somewhere they won't be disturbed."

"That's not the funeral parlor," Polly said. "Frank might drag Hawkins back to our place."

"Too far." He strained to hear a bell ringing mournfully in the darkness.

"Somebody died," he said. "That bell's hanging in front

of Hawkins's mortuary. He must ring it when somebody's died."

"The wind's doing it," Polly said. "Not much of a wind, but enough. He even puts bells on graves, in case he's buried someone alive."

Slocum reflected on how he hadn't been given that chance for release. He had heard of Easterners with a morbid fear of getting stuck underground alive. As fearsome as it was and considering the panic Slocum had experienced, it was a real problem for anyone not dying outright. Some diseases put the person into a coma that wasn't much different from death, only coming out of the coma after burial required some way of letting those aboveground know what had happened.

"The cemetery," Slocum said. "Frank will take him to the cemetery outside town. It's remote and who'd disturb them if he got down to serious torture?"

"I'd stop him from torturing Hawkins," Polly said grimly. "I want my turn at the son of a bitch. Frank shouldn't be so greedy to keep him all to himself."

They rode past the mortuary. Slocum slowed when he saw an indistinct figure slip from the side door and mount. For a moment the light from inside the funeral parlor caught the rider. Slocum couldn't see his face but recognized the battered yellow slicker as belonging to the man who had followed him and Miranda from Dexter Junction.

It took all his willpower not to ride after the man and find who he was.

"Come *on*, John. He's not in there, and you know it."

Polly pointed to the funeral parlor. Slocum relied on his gut, and instinct told him she was right. Hawkins was elsewhere. Their best chance of finding him was to find Frank Neville.

As they turned the corner at the end of the street, heading for the cemetery, Slocum glanced back thinking to catch sight of the slicker-clad stranger. Instead he saw three men dismount in front of the mortuary. One man fell from his horse and had to be supported by a tall, wiry man. The front door opened and spilled forth light. Slocum couldn't tell at this distance but the man supporting his partner matched Polly's description of Julian pretty closely.

If Slocum went back to the funeral home, he could take out all of Hawkins's gang.

"Do I have to ride alone?"

Slocum forced himself to consider other possibilities. He had told Polly that getting rid of Hawkins eliminated the problem. Julian and his men would drift on. Cut the head off the snake. It might not die until sundown, but it would die. All the troubles Polly and her family faced ended if Hawkins died.

He tapped his spurs against his horse's sides and caught up with her. He still worried that leaving behind Julian and his gang, even with the gut-shot man, created a problem hard to deal with later. Worse yet, who was the man in the slicker?

Slocum rode as fast as his horse could go toward the town cemetery. He heard the tinny ringing of bells a ways off. And the evening wind had died down, leaving the sultry night as still as . . . a cemetery.

8

The faint tinkling became indistinct when horses neighed deep within the cemetery. Slocum felt a moment of triumph. He had guessed right what Frank Neville would do, though nothing much else fit into the framework he had constructed. Julian and his gang had arrived at the funeral parlor, but after the mystery man had ridden away. A hell of a lot of firepower spread out behind him if anything went wrong here.

"We can't afford to let Hawkins get away," he told Polly.

From the glare she sent his way, he was preaching to the choir. Slocum made sure his six-shooter rested easy in its holster as he studied the cemetery in front of him. He pointed to the main entrance with a wrought iron arch over the gate. A knee-high picket fence ran the length of the front and disappeared down a slope to either side. The cemetery perched on the top of a low hill.

He slid from the saddle, tied up his horse, and then went to the gate leading into the graveyard. Under the iron arch, he looked up and saw how the dark metal separated one section of sky from another. Ahead lay clouds. Behind, the sky blazed with a million twinkling stars. It struck him as appropriate.

A shriek ahead set him off at a run, pistol clutched in his hand. Polly paced him, her rifle swinging to and fro as she ran.

A moment's silence let through the tinkling bells again. Slocum started toward the sound, but Polly nudged him with the rifle barrel so he looked in a different direction. Two dim figures merged, separated, and once again melted into one giant shadowy being. Slocum recognized the portly Hawkins by his silhouette. It was harder identifying Frank Neville. As he stared at the two men fighting for supremacy, a pistol went off. The muzzle flash momentarily dazzled him and yellow and blue dots bounced about wildly.

Blinking furiously, he cleared his vision and let his longer legs take him up the slope to the gnarled elm tree where one of the men leaned back, clutching his chest.

"Frank!" Polly saw that her brother had been shot before Slocum, no matter that he was in the lead.

Slocum veered away and ran after Hawkins. He should have overtaken the man in a few seconds, but the undertaker knew the layout better than Slocum. Slocum stepped in clumps of cactus and stumbled over unseen tombstones. When he kicked out and his boot met nothing but thin air, he plunged into an open grave. He threw up his arms and smashed his hands against the far side of the grave even as he was bent double until his back threatened to break. A twist turned him belly up to the cloudy night sky. He lay folded up in two for a moment until he caught his breath, then kicked around and stood.

This grave had been dug to the proper depth. His eyes peered along the ground, vision blocked to either side by the mounds of dirt from the grave. He put his hands on the lip and pulled himself up in time to look down a rifle barrel.

"You'd better tell me you left his corpse in that grave, or I swear, I'll put you down there for all eternity."

"He got away," Slocum said, pushing Polly's rifle out of his face. "How's your brother?"

Tears shone like diamonds on the woman's cheeks. Her hands began to shake and she turned away.

Slocum brushed himself off and looked around the cemetery. Wherever Hawkins had gotten off to, he had escaped them. He took the woman's shoulder and turned her back around. For a moment Polly stood as stiff as a statue, then she collapsed into his arms, crying unashamedly.

"He killed my brother. He kidnapped my ma and pa, and he killed Frank. Shot him dead."

"Did your brother say anything about where your folks are?"

"All he said was 'bells.'"

Slocum swung her around and ran off, homing in on the gentle tinkling of bells at two grave sites on a higher hill to the south. When a distant flash of lightning lit the sky, he caught the reflection off two bells held on stakes above graves. Both made feeble ringing noises.

"He put those bell cords down into the coffins," Slocum said, shoving his pistol into his holster and beginning to dig.

The ground was freshly turned, soft, not packed down by weather.

"Get to work on the other grave. This has to be where Hawkins buried your ma and pa."

Polly stood for a moment, then let out a strangled cry that mixed rage and hope into one throat-squeezing sound. She used the stock of her rifle to move dirt away as fast as any prairie dog could dig its burrow on the prairie. Slocum's hands cramped, but he kept them curled into scoops, pulling away large clumps of dirt as well as finer dust and an occasional rock.

They dug furiously for what seemed an eternity. Polly let out a cry of triumph when her rifle stock scrapped across the hidden coffin lid. She abandoned her rifle and used her hands to finish the job. Slocum picked up the rifle and used it the way she had. Before Polly begged him for help pulling the coffin lid up, he had revealed the second casket. He had to choose between helping her and leaving this or continuing.

Slocum slid over, worked his fingers under the nailed-down coffin lid on the far side from Polly. He nodded. Both lifted in unison. The muscles in his forearms corded and threatened to burst from strain. Slocum refused to stop pulling. Nails creaked against the wood, then yielded. He fell back with the lid yanked free. A woman lay in the box.

"The other coffin," he gasped out. "Help me get your pa out now."

Polly hesitated, unsure whether to help her mother or release her father from his wooden prison. She rolled over and got to the far side of the coffin lid so she and Slocum could repeat the lid-opening pull.

The wood cracked and split into pieces. Slocum tossed them aside and bent low. Bubbles on the elder Neville's lips showed he was still alive and struggling to breathe. He pulled the man to a sitting position. This produced a flood of dirt from his nose and mouth. A few gasps and Neville's eyes slowly opened.

"Gotta be heaven. I see my angel."

"Oh, Papa!" Polly threw her arms around him and nearly crushed the wind from his lungs all over again.

Slocum let them cling to each other. Polly had forgotten her mother. He went to the grave and stared down. The woman's dirty lips carried a pale blue tint to them he had seen before in drowned men. Not a muscle twitched. No movement of her eyelids or pulsing of a vein in her throat showed.

"Mama, Mama!"

Slocum caught Polly and swung her around. He held her tight.

"She's dead."

"But the bell. The bell's still ringing and there's no wind and she has to be pulling on that old cord!"

Slocum glanced over his shoulder and saw why the bell

tinkled. A mouse in the coffin gnawed at the string connected to the bell.

"Where's Frank?" Neville struggled over and had to use his daughter for support. "Hawkins killed Marie as sure as the sun rises ever' mornin'. Me and Frank'll fix him for good. Hangin's too good. I ought to—"

"Frank's dead, too, Mr. Neville." Slocum saw no reason to sugarcoat the news. He had to find out eventually. "Hawkins shot him, then ran off. But Frank died trying to get you and his ma free."

"He died a hero, Papa. But Mama—" Polly broke down entirely now, sobbing uncontrollably.

Slocum let her go to her pa so they could share their grief.

He spun, hand flashing to his six-gun, when he heard boots crunching on gravel downhill.

"Don't you throw down on me, boy," the marshal said. He huffed and puffed and waved a shotgun around. If it discharged, there was no telling who would get cut down. "Is that Liam Neville? Where you been, Liam? The whole damned town's been huntin' fer you."

Slocum knew that was a lie. Too many people in Espero disappeared—and all the citizens knew the reason. Leonard Hawkins had his hand in each of those, and his brother was in cahoots.

"Leonard upped and buried me and Marie alive to force me to sign over my ranch. I refused and . . . and Marie died." Neville looked over at the open grave.

"Th-That don't sound like Len," the marshal stammered out.

"Why did you come out here, Marshal?"

Slocum waited for a violent coughing attack to pass before he got in the marshal's face.

"What brought you out here tonight?"

"Some gent came by the office and called out that there was murder goin' on out here. What do you know about that, Slocum?"

"Who was it that warned you?"

Junior Hawkins shook his head, looking a mite worried.

"Never saw who. He was mounted and yelled in at me from out in the street. When I opened the door, he lit out like his horse's tail was on fire. It wasn't. I could see that and—"

"Was he wearing a yellow slicker?"

"You know the varmint, then, Slocum? He surely was. What's happened here?"

"Your brother murdered Frank Neville. His body's over there." Slocum jerked his thumb in the direction of the stunted tree where Frank still lay. "We dug up the Nevilles, but Mrs. Neville was dead. Mr. Neville damned near was, thanks to your brother's murderous ways."

"Now, you don't know it was Len what done all this. You didn't see him good enough, did you, Slocum? You didn't see him shoot down young Neville or bury them two. Why—"

"I'll testify in court that it was him what put me and the missus into our graves," Liam Neville said with hellfire in his voice. "He's gonna pay for that, too. Killin' Frank and Marie and what he done to the rest of this town. He's gonna pay!"

"Settle down now, Liam. You been through hell, from the sound of it, but there's no call for you to talk 'bout takin' the law into your own hands. Get your nerves all quieted 'fore you go makin' threats."

Liam Neville surged. He would have struck the marshal if Slocum hadn't caught him in a bear hug and swung him around so fast his feet left the ground.

"Take you pa back to the ranch," he ordered Polly. "I'll handle this."

"You better, John Slocum. You'd better do right by us Nevilles!" Polly stormed off, almost dragging her father in her wake.

Junior Hawkins took off his hat and mopped his face with his bandanna as Polly and her pa left.

"Much obliged, Slocum. You took care of that real good."

He coughed, then turned and spat out a bloody gob. He wiped his lips with his bandanna before tying it back around his neck. "If there wouldn't be an outcry over it, I'd hire you on as my deputy."

"Do that and the first thing I'd do is bring your brother in."

"Len's not the easiest man to get along with."

"Help me," Slocum said. He didn't wait to see if the marshal followed. He stalked up the hill to where Frank Neville lay slumped over. Bugs of all stripe worked on his carcass in the humid night air.

"What do you want from me?"

"Grab his feet." Slocum got his arms around Neville, then heaved.

The marshal almost keeled over as he took some of the weight of the dead body in both arms. A coughing fit hit him again, but he struggled along as Slocum went to the empty grave where Liam Neville had lain, waiting to die in the suffocating dark. If anything, having the bell to ring made matters worse. If he tugged on the cord, that told Hawkins of complete surrender. But thrashing around in the box, how could Neville not have pulled on the cord?

"We can't go and plant him in somebody's used coffin," protested Hawkins. "That's not right."

Slocum grunted as he dropped Frank into the coffin so recently occupied by his father. He pointed to the coffin lid, which had been broken apart getting Liam Neville free.

"Might go back together," Junior Hawkins muttered.

He began rubbing the broken pieces together until he had the puzzle solved. The lid wasn't solid, but it covered the body. Slocum began scraping the dirt back into the grave. All he had to do was glower to get the marshal to help. It took the better part of twenty minutes before Slocum was satisfied, but he wouldn't let the marshal go. They replaced the lid and dirt on Marie Hawkins's grave.

"Ought to get a preacher out here to say words."

"Wait," Slocum said.

"Fer what?"

"There'll be another grave, but I'm not sure any God-fearing preacher would want to say a prayer over your brother's grave."

"You cain't go 'round threatenin' him like that. You cain't. He's a pillar of the community."

Slocum looked strangely at the marshal. His protests were loud, but his tone carried the opposite meaning.

"You want me to kill your brother for you?"

"I . . . Look, Slocum, I never wanted to be marshal. Len, he put me in the job. I always done what he said ever since I was a little kid." Junior Hawkins swallowed hard, choked, spat, and wiped his mouth with the back of his hand. "When I wasn't more 'n five, he buried me like that." The marshal pointed to Marie Neville's grave. "Only for a few minutes but he promised he'd leave me in the ground if 'n I tole anybody. I . . . I never tole no one till this very second. Truth is, I'm scared of Leonard, damned scared."

"Ride out. Leave. Go to Dexter Junction or Eagle Pass. Hightail it to Mexico. He can't hunt you down if you put enough miles between the two of you."

"You don't know how determined Len is when it comes to family. He would find me. I swear he would. He's got those bully boys ridin' fer him."

"Julian and his gang?"

"Them's the ones. I saw wanted posters on them. There ain't no crime they haven't all done—twice. Look, Slocum, you get rid of Len, and I won't do nothin' to arrest you."

Slocum laughed harshly, as if this pathetic man could arrest anyone wearing a side arm. From the way he coughed up blood and lung, consumption was eating him alive.

"I suppose I could ride off, but it'd be good if I had a trail partner. Me and you, Slocum, we could up and leave Espero. Right now. I don't need nothin' from the office."

"I've got a chore ahead of me. Go back to your office. If I need anything from you, I'll let you know, Marshal."

"Good, glad we had this talk. I . . . I'll be ready to do whatever's needed. In my office. In town."

Junior Hawkins left, stumbling on the uneven path as he made his way downhill. Long after he disappeared into the dark, Slocum heard his coughing and spitting. Slocum walked back to Marie Neville's grave, took off his hat, and said a few words he'd heard over the years. They didn't say much, but he hoped it was enough. He repeated the small service over Frank Neville's grave, then went downhill to the iron arch and passed under it. A weight lifted from his shoulders as he stepped on the far side.

He wished he could depend on the marshal for support, but Junior Hawkins would switch allegiance at the first sign his brother might come out on top. Slocum didn't fool himself. Taking on Hawkins and Julian's gang singlehandedly was going to be tough. As much hate as Polly vented for Hawkins, Slocum let ten times that build in his gut. Hawkins's men had buried him alive, as they had the elder Nevilles. Such evil had to be stopped.

If he had to shoot his way through every hired gunman Leonard Hawkins had in his employ, so be it.

9

He was going to kill him in cold blood.

Slocum shook his head, thinking about that. It really wasn't going to be in cold blood when he killed Leonard Hawkins because he had a festering hatred growing inside him unlike anything he had experienced. Through the years he had drifted across the plains, climbed the Rockies, found death and misery, but John Slocum had never felt this way before. He had been gut-shot by Bloody Bill Anderson for complaining to Quantrill about the viciousness of the Lawrence, Kansas, raid. Boys as young as six had been slaughtered.

He had taken a slug to the gut and had survived. Returning to the family farm in Calhoun, Georgia, had brought new troubles. A carpetbagger judge tried to steal the land. Slocum and buried him and his hired gun down by the springhouse, ridden away, and never looked back. Terrible things had been done to him and those he loved, but never had he felt such seething anger toward another man.

Maybe because those who had wronged him were all dead, his wrath and hatred had been muted. How can anyone hate someone planted six feet down? How could he hate them for long? Justice had been served quickly, without mercy. But now his hand shook thinking about Hawkins and how he took lives in the most cowardly, despicable way imaginable.

The cold dark of the grave should be reserved for those dead, not for the living.

Slocum would shoot his way through Julian's gang to get to the undertaker, if it came to that, but Leonard Hawkins would die.

The clouds moved across the sky, blotting out what star-light there had been. Distant thunder hinted at a new thunderstorm billowing off the Gulf of Mexico to drench the land. A storm was a fitting time for a man to die.

A truly fitting time for Hawkins to die.

A few drops of rain pelted down against Slocum's hat brim. Each splattered wetly and sounded like a lead bullet striking from above. He pulled his hat lower as he came to the funeral parlor. A single light glowed in the room where the caskets were placed on display. Kicking a leg over, Slocum dropped to the ground. He took time to tether his horse out of the rain angling down from the southeast. By the time the storm sent sheets of rain hurtling straight down, he would be done with his chore.

With his vengeance.

Slocum scouted the building, hunting for signs that Julian and his gunmen were still here. He pushed open the front door and slipped inside. Rain dripped from his hat onto the floor, every drop echoing in the stillness. The heavy drapes leading to the viewing room hung slightly open. Through the inch-wide crack came the only light in the building.

Slocum crossed to the velvet drapes and pushed one back using his pistol barrel. He expected to see Leonard Hawkins. Instead, Miranda Madison leaned against a coffin, her head bowed as if in prayer. Slocum moved into the room, kept his back to a solid wall, and watched her.

When she looked up and saw him, she jumped a foot.

Her hand flew to her mouth to cover her outcry. She sagged
down then and said, "John, you startled me. I didn't expect
anyone to be here. No one but . . . him."

She looked back into the coffin.

Slocum walked forward and peered over the edge. The
outlaw he had shot in the gut lay stretched out. If the con-
torted expression etched forever on his face was any indica-
tion, he had died in utter agony from his wound.

"He deserved it," Slocum said.

"What? What do you mean?" Miranda turned from him
to the body and then back. Her hand hid her mouth again.
"You killed him?"

"I wish I had gunned down the three others with him."

"One of them, I think it was the one they called Porkbelly, had been shot in the arm."

Slocum nodded. Polly's marksmanship was decent. He
wished it had been better. One had been killed out on the
road, another lay in the coffin with Slocum's bullet, and
another had a hard time moving because of a shoulder
wound. He had seen Julian and the unscathed outlaw coming into the funeral parlor on his way out to the cemetery.

"Did Julian and the other two leave?"

Miranda nodded. She swallowed hard, then put her hand
on her throat. Her lips moved but only faint sounds came out.

"Where's Hawkins?"

"You're going to kill him?"

"Is he here?"

"You can't shoot him. John! We're getting married
tomorrow."

"I don't want to make you a widow. I'll cut him down
tonight."

"I'm begging you, don't. Let him be. Let me marry him.
I have to!"

Slocum stared at her. She was earnest, and her eyes
welled with tears at the idea of Hawkins being put into one
of his caskets.

"You don't know what he's done, what he's capable of doing. A woman like you can marry any man she wants."

Miranda snorted in contempt. Her lip curled and she shook her head vigorously, her hair spun out from her face and formed an auburn halo that made her all the more beautiful. If only she didn't look as if she was going to bite him.

"You don't know what I've gone through. Please, trust me. Believe me when I say I want to marry him."

"Where is he?"

"I don't know. It's bad luck for the groom to see the bride on the night before the wedding. Leonard said he was going to spend his night somewhere else. With one of his brothers perhaps."

Slocum knew Hawkins wasn't with the marshal. That left the bank president's house as the likeliest refuge for the undertaker after the fight at the cemetery.

"Where does the bank president live?"

"Kenneth? I don't know. I was only introduced to him this afternoon. He was quite brusque."

"That's the bank president?"

"Yes, Kenneth Hawkins. He is going to be his brother's best man. Tomorrow. Or is it today? Time is getting away from me."

"Crying over dead outlaws can do that," Slocum said. "You know him?"

"No." Miranda looked confused at the sudden turn. "I don't really know anyone in Espero."

Slocum started to mention the man wearing the oilcloth slicker, then held back. A crash of thunder masked another sound, a softer noise. Water dripped onto a floor somewhere else—and a puff of wind from outside moved the heavy velvet curtains. He swung his six-gun away from the woman and trained it on the drapes just as a shotgun barrel pushed the heavy material aside.

Slocum and the man with the shotgun fired at the same instant. The shotgun blast tore away part of the coffin.

Slocum's bullet flew straight and true. As the man crashed forward, pulling the drapery with him, Slocum saw he had finished the job Polly had begun out on the road. The man dead on the floor had his right arm bandaged up and held in a sling. Using a shotgun had been his only option. Wielding it left-handed—clumsily—spelled his death.

"You killed him," Miranda said in a small voice. "Just like that, you shot him down."

Slocum hardly listened. He swung around the doorway, six-shooter trained on the outer lobby. The door to the street swung to and fro as the growing storm wind clutched at it. A quick look outside showed only one horse. Slocum ducked back inside and secured the door with a locking bar.

Miranda waited for him in the viewing room. She had taken a chair to the side, hands folded in her lap. She looked more composed than before. Adapting to a pair of corpses in the same room had come easily for her, Slocum thought.

"Why'd he come back?"

"Leonard might have sent him to be my bodyguard. He said something this afternoon about someone wanting to harm him through me. That is pure fantasy, of course."

"Yeah, pure fantasy," Slocum said. He slid his Colt back into its holster, grabbed the man on the floor by the collar, and dragged him across the floor, leaving a thin trail of sticky blood behind. Getting his feet under him, Slocum heaved and got the man upright. "Help me," he said. He had found out the hard way why the man's moniker was Porkbelly.

"What are you going to do?"

"Two to a coffin's still more than they deserve."

Miranda grabbed the outlaw's feet and guided them up over the edge of the coffin. Slocum dropped the man on top of the other. Then he searched the man's pockets and found only a silver dollar. He pocketed it, much to Miranda's disgust.

"Do you always rob men you've just slaughtered?"

"When they stole all my money before burying me alive,

yeah," Slocum said. "Somebody still owes me for escorting you to Espero."

"But Leonard paid you . . ." Her voice trailed off. Her lips thinned and she looked at him like a mother scolding her young 'un. "You aren't saying Leonard had anything to do with that robbery, are you? That's absurd. And burying a man alive? That's why he provides the bells for many of his customers. He told me about a story by some Baltimore writer named Poe. 'Premature Burial,' the man wrote. Leonard said he would read it to me after we are married so I can better understand his business."

Thunder crashed outside. A momentary flash of lighting lit the room a dozen times brighter than the oil lamp on the table. Slocum studied Miranda's face and again marveled at her beauty. And her gullibility believing she had a life with Leonard Hawkins. Even a brief talk with the man ought to have sent her galloping away as fast as she could ride.

"Where's the wedding supposed to be?"

"There's a barn at the far end of town. I'm not sure who will perform the ceremony since Leonard said the preacher had died some time ago and Espero never replaced him. He told me he had requested a circuit preacher, but I don't know if he's arrived. There might be a judge in town. Whoever it is marrying us, Leonard promised me it would be legal."

Slocum wondered at the woman's concern for the marriage being official when she was marrying a vicious killer. But she remained oblivious to that, no matter how the evidence piled up around him. Slocum glanced at the two corpses. Even those deaths did nothing to spook her.

"You'll be all right. I need to find Kenneth Hawkins."

"Wait. The rain. The storm's getting worse. Stay. Please." She came out of her chair and grasped his arm rightly enough that he had to yank away to break her grip. "I don't want to be alone tonight, John."

He couldn't fathom what she was asking of him. It sounded as if she intended him to share her bed, but everything

Miranda said spoke of her devotion to Leonard Hawkins. How being cuckolded the night before his wedding would set with the undertaker hardly occurred to Slocum. What did make him wonder was the woman's attitude.

"If I can't find him tonight, I'll be at the barn for the wedding."

"John, please. I'm begging you. Don't hurt Leonard. Let me marry him."

He evaded her grasp again and stepped across the bloody trail on the floor. There would be more blood spilled before the night was over if he found Hawkins.

He closed the outer door against her pleas to let Hawkins be. The fury of the storm sending down sheets of rain suited him better. The storm had moved quickly and drove raindrops straight down. His good intentions putting his pinto in the lee of the wind had been for nothing. He swung up into the creaking, wet saddle and rode into the rain, wiping rivers from his eyes as he went up one street and down another hunting for the bank. When he found it, his hopes soared.

A house attached to the rear of the bank might be Kenneth Hawkins's living quarters. Slocum wondered if the banker had the same dedication to money that his brother did to death. It was almost too much to hope that Kenneth Hawkins viewed banking the same way his youngest brother did law enforcement.

Dismounting, Slocum went to a window and peered inside. A kerosene lamp put out a sputtering yellow light. The lamp's wick needed trimming. In fact, the whole shabby house needed renovation. The furniture was in disrepair, and the cupboard door hung on one hinge, revealing a sparse larder. Hawkins might not live here, but the almost full lamp burned, showing someone had been here recently.

Slocum went to the door and lifted the latch. He shoved, but the door resisted. The rain had caused the wood to swell. Putting his shoulder to the door bought him swift entry. Keeping his gun roving around the room as he sought a target, he took in more of the furnishings. A bank president living in squalor like this boggled the mind.

He crossed the small room and poked through a trunk filled with quilts and a man's clothing. Slocum turned slowly when he heard movement behind him. His pistol lifted to center on Kenneth Hawkins's midsection.

"What are you, a sneak thief? I don't have anything to steal!"

"Come in and close the door." Slocum motioned with his six-gun for the banker to sit in one of the two chairs at the table. "What is this place?"

"What's it look like? This is my home."

Slocum hid his surprise. Hawkins sounded truthful.

"You don't believe I can live like this?" The bitterness told more than the words. "Leonard doesn't believe that bankers deserve to be paid well. Or hardly at all. The boy sweeping up at the general store makes more than I do. I know; I loaned old man Bennett enough to keep him going when business died down here." Hawkins looked at Slocum. "The railroad went to Dexter Junction, not to Espero."

"All that's left here is ranching."

"And some farming, of course."

Slocum waved the six-gun about to indicate the house.

"Why do you stay if your brother owns the bank and won't let you earn a decent wage?"

Kenneth Hawkins turned pale. He wiped rain from his face with a hand shaking so badly he might have palsy.

"You don't know Leonard. He's not like other men. His interests are strange and dangerous—for everyone else."

"I know he buried the Nevilles alive to force Liam Neville to sign over the deed to the Box N."

Hawkins closed his eyes as his lips moved in a silent prayer. He heaved a deep breath and looked at Slocum.

"I'm sorry. I didn't know."

"The hell you didn't. You're no fool. You know what he's doing to this town."

"Nothing he hasn't done before. You asked why I stay. That gang following his every whim."

"You can get away. It's not as if you would be leaving much behind." Slocum looked around the room. The quilts and clothing in the single chest were worth more than the rest of the possessions combined, with the house itself thrown in for good measure.

"He would catch me. And if he did . . ."

"What would he do to you?"

"The same as he did to our parents. The same as he did to the Nevilles."

Slocum almost pulled the trigger to put the man out of his misery.

"He buried *your* ma and pa alive?"

"He sat under a tree on the hill reading a story aloud, as if they could hear it."

"Something by this Poe fellow?"

Hawkins's eyebrows arched in surprise.

"Leonard is quite a reader. He reads everything he can find if it has to do with death, burials, and funeral rituals. He forced me to sit and listen as he read 'A Cask of Amontillado' and then 'Premature Burial.' It took him the better part of an afternoon. When we left, they had been buried for more than two hours. There wasn't any way they could have been alive."

Hawkins looked around, then smiled without a trace of humor. "He made me read another story to him. 'The Tell-Tale Heart.' I swear I hear their screams in the night and have ever since I was seven."

"If you had any gumption, you would get a gun and shoot the son of a bitch."

"I couldn't. His eyes are like knives, piercing your soul. He knows what I'm thinking before I do."

"You should have shot him in the back, then," Slocum

said in distaste. "He's a monster and preys on other people's fears."

"He's gotten fat off mine," Kenneth Hawkins admitted.

"Where is he?"

"You mean to shoot him down?"

"Like the mad dog that he is," Slocum said. "Where is he?"

"I don't know. If I did, believe me, I would tell you. If you spooked him, he's probably with Julian. If there's anyone more vicious than my brother, it's him. They see enough of themselves in the other that they've become fast friends."

Slocum suspected that all Leonard Hawkins wanted was power. He shared freely the ill-gotten spoils of his extortion and outright robbery with Julian. Men like that sought money, not power, because a town eventually got up enough backbone in its citizens to have a necktie party. Why the people of Espero hadn't done that with Hawkins was something he didn't need to explore. They hadn't.

He would.

"Where do Julian and his gang camp when they're in town? Is there a hotel? A saloon where they hang out?"

"I never heard. They might be at the hotel since Leonard owns it. The saloon, too." Kenneth Hawkins smiled his rueful smile and added, "He almost gives the drinks away. That keeps the people drunk and from getting too frisky."

"You're his best man?"

"The wedding? Yes, I am. Tomorrow morning at nine A.M. sharp."

"Where?"

Kenneth knew Slocum's interest. If Leonard or the gang couldn't be found tonight, the wedding gave the best chance of gunning down the undertaker.

"There's a barn behind the livery stable that hasn't been used for anything more 'n barn dances this past year. That's where Leonard's going to tie the knot."

That jibed with what Miranda had told him. Slocum got up to leave, paused, and had to ask a final question.

"Why's she marrying him?"

He hadn't expected an answer and didn't get one from the banker. Some questions might not have answers, and this was one of them. He pushed out into the storm, intent on finding the hotel in the hope that Leonard Hawkins slept there. The sooner he died, the sooner the town would be free and Slocum could move on.

10

The banker wasn't wrong.

"I'll have another," Slocum said, pushing his nickel across the bar and getting another shot of whiskey. It wasn't the best he had ever swilled, but it was good enough and was just what he needed. Horace just stared at him. After the first time in the Six Feet Under when Slocum had expertly identified the whiskey's content, the formula had been changed. Slocum didn't detect the nitric acid in this batch.

"I remember you. You're the gent what brung Mr. Hawkins's new missus to town, aren't you? The one with Max when he was gunned down?" The barkeep hitched up his drawers and rearranged the apron tied around his ample middle.

Slocum nodded, tasted the whiskey, letting it burn his lips. A quick movement sent the entire ounce down his throat. It warmed him when he needed something cool against the humid night, but the calming effect of the alcohol was worth the heat.

"You still workin' for him?"

Slocum looked up sharply. The man's apprehension told Slocum how fully Leonard Hawkins controlled this town.

"Can't say I am. Just staying for the wedding."

Horace relaxed a mite, working on restacking the shot glasses behind the bar.

"You better be ready for a big wingding. Mr. Hawkins has been talkin' about his new wife ever since that first time she writ back. This is a cause for real celebration in Espero. Yes, sir, it is."

"There's no need to convince yourself of that," Slocum said.

"What do you mean?"

"I know he owns this saloon and damned near everything else in town. I know how he keeps everyone under his thumb, you included."

"You're talkin' crazy, mister." The barkeep moved away, taking an occasional look over his shoulder as if Slocum had grown horns and a spade tail.

Slocum ran his finger around the rim of the glass, then licked the last drop off. At the prices charged, he could buy an entire bottle for fifty cents and not go blind drinking it. Rather than ask for another, Slocum let the water drip off him onto the sawdust covering the floor. He hadn't found Hawkins anywhere. The man knew the town—hell, he *owned* the town—and after the dustup out at the cemetery, he was likely to lie low for a spell. Considering he went ahead with his wedding in the morning, he might be in bed somewhere with a whore.

That thought made Slocum shudder. What would he do to a soiled dove who didn't pleasure him enough? What would he do to Miranda if she failed in her wifely duties? A man with the twisted tastes of the undertaker undoubtedly had appetites no normal woman could satisfy. Saying he would make her a coffin as a wedding present might only be the start.

His search through the rain-drenched streets had failed

to turn up Julian and his gang, too. Hawkins might be holed up with them, fearing not only Slocum but Liam Neville and his daughter. This brought a smile to Slocum's lips. He knew nothing about Polly's pa, but he had seen how determined she was. Losing her brother and ma made her all the more dangerous to Hawkins. She wouldn't care about the law, about trials or anything but getting her revenge.

He moved his hand closer to his Colt Navy as he vowed to beat her to Leonard Hawkins. Polly had been wronged, but she hadn't been buried alive. Slocum caught his breath as he remembered the darkness, the closed-in pine walls, the air turning worse with every breath he took.

To cover his remembered discomfort, Slocum started to call out to the barkeep. He glanced into the mirror behind the bar and saw a pair of men pushing their way into the saloon. One made a beeline for the bar to order. The other, thinner man hung back to scout out everyone in the room. His head looked as if it had gotten caught between an anvil and a smithy's hammer, but it was the scar on the left cheek that confirmed Slocum's suspicion. This was Julian, the man who had buried him alive.

Slocum turned away from the barkeep so his hand could move easily to his six-shooter. He kept turning, whirled about, and leveled his Colt.

Julian had anticipated the move and had ducked back into the night.

Slocum kept spinning around and got the drop on the man who had come in with Julian. He caught him with the shot glass in his hand rather than a six-shooter.

"Move and you're dead," Slocum said.

The outlaw dropped his glass with a loud ringing sound. It hit the bar and spun about. The shot glass caught light from the gas lamp on the wall behind the bar and flashed. This distraction was enough to keep Slocum from squeezing the trigger.

Julian poked his pistol back through the door and opened

fire. Slocum fired, missed Julian's partner, and then dived over the bar to keep from taking a slug flung his way by the gang leader.

"My bar! You're shootin' it to splinters! My bar—" Horace grabbed his head with both hands and cried out in dismay.

That was all the protest the barkeep got out before the man he had just served cut him down. Slocum hunkered down with bullets tearing through the wood between him and the doorway. One exploded a bottle in front of him, showering him with glass and whiskey. Again distracted, he almost died. The man at the far end of the bar jumped over. If he hadn't stumbled on the body of the saloon keeper he had just murdered, he would have drilled Slocum. As it was, the slug went high.

Slocum's return fire was on target. He drove three bullets into the man's chest. When he refused to die, Slocum had only one choice. He used his last bullet on the man. This one hit him in the head.

More bullets slammed into the bar, some penetrating to create more havoc behind. From the sheer amount of lead, more than one man had to be firing. The rest of Julian's gang had joined him in his assault.

Slocum reloaded. Staying where he was spelled eventual death. He wiggled on his belly through the spilled whiskey and broken glass to grab up the dead outlaw's six-shooter. Slocum popped up from behind the bar and emptied it at the doorway. He was rewarded with a yelp that told him he winged one of his attackers. It wasn't a killing shot, but it would keep Julian and his men at bay for a few seconds.

With a quick vault, Slocum hit the floor on the far side of the bar. His boots slid out from under him as he found sawdust rather than solid footing. This saved his life. Through the window came a rain of lead that would have cut him in half if he had stayed on his feet. He spun about and made his way on hands and knees to an overturned table. The other customers in the saloon had wisely lit out, leaving Slocum and the Julian gang to shoot it out.

The tabletop began splintering away as the bullets bored into it. When a shotgun blast hit the table, it sent both what remained of the wood and Slocum sliding toward the back of the room.

"You quit shootin', dammit!"

Slocum recognized the marshal's voice.

"You cain't go shootin' up my brother's saloon like this."

The dull crunch of metal striking bone warned Slocum that the lawman wasn't going to press his complaint any further. Julian had buffaloed him.

The small diversion let Slocum dive for the back room. He slid in amid new rounds coming his way. Wasting no time, he got to his feet and the back at the same time. He shouldered open the door and fired point-blank into a man with a drawn six-shooter. At this range Slocum could not miss. The gunman went down without so much as a peep.

Slocum ran for the next building. The rear door was locked. He kept going until he was far enough from the saloon to simply step into a doorway and let the shadows conceal him. Up and down the alley roamed three men with rifles. They yelled at each other futilely and finally gave up.

"Julian ain't gonna like it how we let him get away."

"It was Reilly's fault." The sound of a boot kicking the man Slocum had shot dead echoed down the alley. "We kin blame it all on him."

"We better or Julian'll skin us alive."

"That's still better 'n what that loco weed that's payin' us would do."

Slocum waited a few more seconds before peering out. The alley was deserted. Even the downed man had been removed. He made his way to a space between two stores and edged toward the main street. He froze. Julian and four men rode past, not looking in his direction. Two other horses carried bodies draped over their saddles.

He had gone to the saloon intending to track down Leonard Hawkins. The man might be hiding with the gang he paid so handsomely, but rather than track the retreating outlaws, Slocum returned to the saloon. Junior Hawkins moaned and struggled to sit up.

Slocum swung him around and pushed the man against the wall for support.

"You," the marshal said. He started to curse, coughed, and turned to spit out half his lungs. Not bothering to wipe his mouth, he looked back at Slocum. "That was you in there, wasn't it?"

"Where's Julian and his gang holed up? With your brother?"

This caused the marshal to sharpen his look. He nodded.

"If you want your brother removed permanently, tell me where Julian is going."

"Don't know. Honest, Slocum. I meant it when I said Leonard'll be the death of me."

"That consumption is going to kill you real soon."

"And I damned well don't want Len buryin' me neither! He'd do it 'fore my body was cold and then laugh over my grave. He's like that."

"Where's Julian likely to go?" Slocum watched the marshal carefully. The man knew. "Where? Your brother's with him."

Just saying those words tightened Slocum's gut. Find Julian, find Hawkins, and exact his revenge.

"There's a hollow outside town where he'd go. You'd never find it. Help me up, will you?"

Slocum grabbed Junior Hawkins's hand and dragged him to his feet. The man was lighter than he looked. The consumption had eaten away his innards and taken most of his muscle, leaving only a husk.

"Gotta show you—otherwise you'd never find it."

Slocum watched the marshal go on shaky legs to fetch his horse. With a single vault, he mounted his own and walked alongside the marshal all the way back to the jail-house. The lawman saddled his horse and mounted, then set off down Espero's main street without a backward look to see if Slocum trailed him.

It wasn't the bravest thing in the world, but Slocum kept a dozen yards behind the marshal. If Junior Hawkins alerted any of Julian's sentries, he would be the first to draw fire, giving Slocum a chance to locate and kill any dry-gulchers. A mile outside town, the marshal cut off the road and went along a trail hardly large enough to be seen in the dark. In the woods on either side, small creatures complained at this invasion.

Slocum saw eyes of animals that could never be called small. He drew his Winchester and laid it across the saddle in front of him, ready for anything from Julian to a rampaging javelina.

"Hey, boss, it's me, Junior!"

The marshal's voice came muffled and distant, though he was hardly twenty yards away. Slocum brought up his rifle, snugging it to his shoulder. Only then did he tap his horse's flanks to narrow the distance between him and the marshal.

He saw Marshal Hawkins ahead, hands up in the air to show he wasn't here to cause any trouble.

"I need to talk with my brother."

"He's not here, Junior."

The gravelly voice cut across Slocum's senses. That had to be Julian answering. He rode closer, alert for guards on the trail hidden in the thicket around him. A small rustling noise distracted him. He swung his rifle around to cover a rabbit. This small move spelled disaster ahead.

"Don't shoot, dammit. I'm—" That was as far as the marshal got before the woods lit up with a half-dozen lances of flame from pistols and rifles.

Slocum leaned forward and put his weight on his horse's shoulders to prevent it from rearing. He fired at the nearest spot where he knew an outlaw hid. His shot produced a groan. A good shot, but not a killing one. He brought up his rifle and fired into a cluster of gunmen. When the magazine came up empty, he drew his six-gun.

Only he sat astride his horse in the dark forest, isolated, the smell of gunsmoke in his nostrils. Through the ringing in his ears, he heard horses galloping away. Slocum had only two choices, advance or retreat through the pitch-black woods. He let out a rebel yell and charged.

Bursting into a clearing, he saw how fast Julian and his men had abandoned their camp. The cooking fire was still heating a pot of coffee. Blankets were spread out where the outlaws had intended to sleep. And two horses had been left tied to a rope strung between two honey locust trees. As quick as the search of the camp was, Slocum saw where the gang had fled through the woods. The ground was cut up where a half-dozen horses had run.

He slowed, circled the clearing, and finally stopped. Chasing the outlaw gang all by himself was complete idiocy. They had run because they thought the marshal had brought a posse with him. That was the only reason Slocum could think for their hasty retreat.

Julian must have expected the marshal to cross him after he had been clubbed in town. Slocum hunted the camp for any trace left by Leonard Hawkins. If the undertaker had been here, his spoor mingled perfectly with that left by the others in the gang. Disgusted, Slocum kicked a dirt clod into the nearby fire, where it sputtered and almost extinguished the flames. Blazing bravely, the fire returned.

Slocum went to it, pulled the coffeepot off the fire, and found a tin cup abandoned nearby. He drank a cup, approving of whoever had fixed the coffee. That didn't mean Slocum wouldn't cut the man down the first chance he got, but he did make a fine pot of joe.

He searched the saddlebags and other belongings left behind, taking what money he found. It still came up several hundred short of what Hawkins had paid him and then stole back. Finished and disgusted that he hadn't found the undertaker, Slocum looked around. His eyes finally fixed on the black notch in the woods and the trail leading back to where Junior Hawkins lay gunned down. Several seconds passed as Slocum considered what to do. He finally trudged along the trail, grabbed the dead marshal under the arms, and dragged his body into the clearing.

"He won't get you," Slocum said softly.

He began digging in the soft forest and worked diligently until he had a hole five feet deep. Going deeper wasn't in the cards since he hit a layer of white caliche that would take dynamite to blast through. He wrapped Junior Hawkins up in a couple blankets left by the outlaws, rolled the body into the hole, then returned the dirt to the grave.

More than an hour later, Slocum stared at the mounded dirt. Putting a marker on the grave only invited trouble should Leonard Hawkins see it. The chances against that were high. Slocum sat, carved the name into a broad wood limb, then affixed it as a crosspiece to another stuck down into the dirt. It wasn't much but more than the marshal likely deserved.

For Slocum, he felt some small satisfaction at robbing Leonard Hawkins of another body to feed his sick pleasures.

As he turned, he saw movement at the far side of the clearing, near the notch in the woods where Julian and the gang had escaped. He slid his Colt free and tried not to be too obvious that he had discovered the intruder as he made his way to his horse.

A rifle spoke. Dirt kicked up at Slocum's feet.

"Freeze, mister," came the shouted command. "If you twitch a muscle, I'll kill you."

Slocum had been caught away from any useful shelter against an ambush. He obeyed.

"You're not one of the gang. They killed the marshal."

"I saw you burying him. That the one they call Junior Hawkins?"

"Is," Slocum affirmed.

"You get on the road to Dexter Junction and keep on going. There's nothing for you here but a quick death."

"You're the one who's been following me, the one who wears the yellow slicker."

This caused the man to gasp. He covered quickly and said, "There's nothing for you in Espero. Get out while you can."

"Why don't you just gun me down?"

"I don't have a quarrel with you."

"You mean Miranda doesn't."

Slocum feinted to his left and dived right as a bullet sang past. He landed hard on his belly and wiggled fast toward a fallen tree trunk. Bullets whined overhead, but the man's aim was off in the darkness. Slocum made sure he didn't present such a fine target again. He aimed his six-shooter in the direction of the rifle fire, then waited. When another muzzle flash showed, he would fire just a little bit under it.

Only no bullets came his way now. Slocum waited a few minutes, listening hard and hearing only the nocturnal animals slowly recovering their disturbed duties in the surrounding woods. He worked his way slowly around the edge of the clearing, avoiding the worst of the thicket while still using the trees as cover until he reached the spot where a couple bits of shiny brass caught his eye.

Bending low, he grabbed one. The case was still warm from being fired. Finding boot prints or other spoor in the detritus on the floor of the woods proved impossible in the dark. Slocum moved in the direction most likely taken by his ambusher, found a couple hoofprints in the soft ground, and then holstered his six-gun.

Once more he was alone in the woods. And he had no idea where Leonard Hawkins, his gang, or the man who had followed Miranda Madison from Dexter Junction were.

11

There were too many of them. Slocum spotted six armed men strategically posted around the barn where the nuptials were going to be held. Slipping inside the barn unseen would take more skill than Slocum possessed. Through the open doors, he caught sight of white bunting and folded paper bells decorating the walls and dangling over the altar set up at the far end of the barn where stalls had been ripped out.

He considered the distance and what chance he had making a shot using his rifle. To kill Leonard Hawkins as he stood there waiting for his bride to appear held no appeal for Slocum. He wanted the man to know whose hand brought about his death. Even hanging wasn't good enough for him, but Slocum would agree to that if he could open the trapdoor under the undertaker's feet.

If there had been a lawman left in Espero. If a judge could be found or a jury convened that didn't owe Hawkins their livelihoods and even their families' lives. If, if, if . . .

Bringing in the Rangers hardly seemed adequate, even if they chose to interest themselves in Hawkins's crimes. Finding enough proof that he had caused anyone's death to bring a roving lawman into Espero looked out of the question. Slocum had a distaste for lynch mobs, and taking the law into his own hands smacked of that. At the same time, it didn't. If proof that would stand up in court against Hawkins wasn't available, Slocum had no trouble becoming judge, jury, and executioner.

Only this wasn't the place where he could be the executioner. The angle and distance were too great, even for a marksman of his ability.

He settled down on the roof of a bookstore a hundred yards away from the barn, studying the growing crowd with his field glasses. Three more men whose allegiance to Julian looked obvious showed up. Hawkins had brought in a small army of outlaws to protect himself today. He needed it.

Slocum wondered whether his desire to personally make Hawkins aware of who brought him slow, painful death rested on his desire for revenge or what Miranda Madison had said when he found her in the funeral parlor. She had begged him not to harm Hawkins and to let the marriage continue. He felt some obligation to her. Delivering any woman into the arms of a man like Hawkins had to rankle. But she knew him by now—she had to.

She still wanted to marry him.

The man in the yellow slicker added to the mystery. Slocum knew the man had spoken with Miranda more than once since she had come to Espero. If he was a jilted suitor, he certainly acted strangely. He had a better chance to shoot down Hawkins than Slocum, yet the night before he had only tried to chase him off rather than kill him by summoning the marshal. Only when Slocum had angered him had the man fired. And that anger came from hinting that he did nothing but Miranda's bidding.

Was Slocum any different if he didn't shoot Hawkins before the ceremony?

He slowly scanned across the crowd when they began to move forward to get into the barn. He located six of Julian's henchmen herding the townspeople inside as if they were nothing more than balky sheep. That image came easily for Slocum. If the citizens had ever once united against Hawkins, he wouldn't hold them in slavery now, doing his bidding. Gaining the deeds to the surrounding ranches and farms had come only after he'd secured his foothold in the town.

Hadn't even one of the town's upstanding citizens tried to gun him down after a loved one had been spirited off for living burial? Fear could grip a town only so long until anger built.

Or had the fear became such a part of everyone's thoughts that they buckled to any demand, no matter how small or absurd?

From what Slocum had seen, Hawkins was shrewd about how he wielded his power. Cheap whiskey went a ways toward keeping everyone in line. He thought on what he had seen around Espero. There weren't any obvious cathouses. If Hawkins closed them down and ran off the soiled doves, the town's respectable women might be less inclined to oppose him.

Slocum tensed when he saw a tight group of men moving at the far side of the barn. He trained his field glasses on the man in the center. Leonard Hawkins was dressed in solid black. His morning coat seemed to swallow the sun's brightness. Satin stripes down the sides of his pants provided only a small hint of frivolity. He sported a solid black vest, a black shirt, and a cravat held in place by a headlight diamond that, when the light caught it, became a jealous rival to the sun itself. Hawkins wore a tall silk top hat and spun an ebony cane about in his hand. The gold knob flashed like a beacon until he disappeared into the barn.

Slocum considered dropping the field glasses and taking up his rifle when he saw Julian and two henchmen huddle together. If he couldn't take out Hawkins, removing his top ally would go a ways toward reaching the undertaker later. As he raised his Winchester, Slocum stopped. Julian ducked back inside the barn while the two outlaws he had spoken to ran off in the direction of the bank.

Following the pair with his binoculars confirmed Slocum's suspicion as to their mission. They went around to the small shack where Kenneth Hawkins lived. A few minutes later, they frog-marched the banker out and back to the barn, where the crowd waited with growing impatience. The banker struggled, but the two held his arms pinned behind him until they were met by Julian.

Reading lips was a skill Slocum had never learned, but he didn't have to know what was said to understand how it beat down the banker's resistance. The two outlaws released his arms; they fell limp to his sides. He refused to look up until Julian grabbed him by the throat, shoved his face within inches of the banker's, and spoke rapidly. When he finished, he shoved Kenneth Hawkins back and waited.

Beaten, the banker went into the barn. From his narrow field of vision through the door, Slocum saw Hawkins take his place as best man in front of the dais. Julian came up behind, shoved something into Hawkins's grip, and backed away.

Leonard Hawkins joined his brother, pried open the man's fist to see what Julian had placed there, nodded once briskly, then turned to face the altar set up on the dais. From the single sparkle, a diamond ring of considerable size had been given to the best man in preparation for the ceremony.

Music came up from inside. Slocum had heard the wedding march enough times to recognize it and how off-key it was being played. The piano player from the saloon must be banging out the tune. No chorus inside sang or other music billowed out from the barn.

Slocum came upright when he saw a buggy rattle up and stop a few feet from the open double doors. He didn't recognize the driver, but the man wore a fancy coat and donned a gray top hat before helping Miranda down. Slocum caught his breath when he saw how lovely she was, bathed in warm sunlight, her brilliant white dress such a contrast to her groom's attire, and the soft haze of pearls around her throat. The man extended his arm, and she took it to enter.

Whoever this was, he stood in for her father to give away the bride.

She paused at the double doors, then gracefully walked the length of the barn to stand beside Hawkins in front of the altar. A man came into Slocum's view, mostly hidden by the barn door's lintel. He saw a Bible open and fingers flipping through to find the proper page. The marriage was under way.

Too far to hear what was being said, Slocum only guessed at the process. By now the question of anyone objecting to the marriage had been asked. If anyone had, Slocum knew bullets would have flown. Julian would have no compunction against following Hawkins's orders to cut down anyone objecting. But who in town could object? No one here knew Miranda.

No one but the man who had followed her here from Dexter Junction.

As that crossed his mind, Slocum caught movement out of the corner of his eye. Two men scuffled in the street. Slocum focused the field glasses on them. As they traded blows, he saw that one of them was the mystery man dogging Miranda Madison's every step. But the other got Slocum moving from his position on the bookstore roof. He grabbed his rifle, rolled over the peak in the roof, and slid down the street side, tearing off shingles as he went.

Slocum landed hard in the street, recovered his dropped rifle, and ran toward the two fighting. Miranda's secret admirer had already taken the worst of it. Liam Neville fought with the fury of ten men and had knocked the other man senseless.

"Neville, don't!" Slocum shouted. Liam Neville looked around, his eyes wild and crazy. When he saw Slocum, he dragged out a pistol and got off a shot that came uncomfortably close. Slocum kept running. "They'll kill you. There're too many of them inside!"

Liam Neville ignored him and ran for the barn where the wedding was in its final phases. Slocum had too much ground to cover to reach the wild man before he bulled on into the barn.

"I'm going to kill you for what you done, Leonard Hawkins!"

Slocum got off a shot that dropped one of Julian's gang before he could fire on Neville. But too many others were inside. And others came around the barn from the far side. Slocum knelt and began firing as accurately as he could, taking out those outside the barn. From the corner of his eye, he saw Leonard Hawkins grab his brother's wrist and force open his hand. He snatched the wedding ring and savagely screwed it down onto Miranda's finger.

The wedding was official with the final, "I now pronounce you man and wife."

No cheers sounded in the barn. The crowd might have been assembled for a funeral rather than a wedding. Gunfire outside might have held down their enthusiasm, but Slocum thought it was more likely lack of fondness for Leonard Hawkins.

He drove back three more of Julian's gunmen and saw Liam Neville push aside two women as he made his way into the barn.

"You have killed the only woman I have ever loved, Hawkins, and I'll return the favor!"

Slocum saw the flare of a lucifer and the sputter of a miner's fuse. Neville held up a bundle of dynamite sticks tied together with rope. From the length of the fuse, it would detonate in less than ten seconds. Not even thinking, Slocum dug in his toes and sprinted for the barn. The crowd poured out, making it hard for him to get inside.

Neville reared back and threw the dynamite. The resounding explosion a second later knocked Slocum off his feet. He hit, rolled, and returned to fighting his way inside. The dynamite had blown away the back half the barn. Throughout the crowd, men and women moaned, cried in pain, fought to regain their senses.

Slocum wrapped his arms around Liam Neville and threw him from the barn. The half still standing let out a mournful creak and groan as it began collapsing slowly. Slocum saw so many others around him needing help. All he could do was get himself out from under the thick wooden beams falling downward now that the supports had been wrecked.

He got away an instant before the barn fell in on itself. Neville stood staring at the havoc he had wrought. One ear had been sheared off by the blast. The eye on that side of his face was missing, speared by a flying splinter. Blood and ichor ran down his cheek. Burns on the rest of his face would soon blister. Slocum spared the man nothing as he grabbed him up again and carried him away. From the feel, ribs had been shattered and the tattered, burned clothing hid similarly ruined flesh.

Neville began crying out in agony. Slocum tossed him into the buggy Miranda had ridden to her wedding in. Scooping up the reins, he got the horse pulling. The shrieks of pain from the survivors added speed to the frightened horse's effort. The buggy wheels sang as the horse broke into a wild gallop. Slocum knew something had to break soon. The buggy hadn't been built to take either the weight or the speed Slocum inflicted on it. He slowed, looked back into town, and realized he was fleeing when no one pursued.

How long would it take for Julian's men to come after them? Slocum realized many of the gang had been killed or wounded in the explosion. Hell, most of the town had to be included in that number.

He slowed but kept the buggy headed out of town. Not knowing where he went caused him to slow even more until he saw a painted sign pointing the way to the Box N Ranch. Slocum turned down the road and kept driving until well after noon. As he approached the ranch house, he grew warier. A single curl of smoke came from the chimney. The walls had been shot up and the barn had been burned to the ground. He had seen farmhouses in Virginia during the war that hadn't taken this much damage.

It was too late to turn around, but he looked for a way to get the buggy under cover if those responsible for the destruction were still inside.

"Where are we?"

Slocum looked at Neville. The man had moaned in pain most of the way but hadn't spoken. He pulled the man upright to let him peer out with his one good eye. Slocum wasn't sure how much he saw, but the sight of the Box N ranch house buoyed Neville's spirits.

"Home," was all he said.

"Hands up!" came the harsh order from the front porch.

Polly Neville held up a double-barreled shotgun and looked ready to use it.

"Hold your horses," Slocum called. "I got your pa here, and he's hurt real bad."

"John? How'd you get him? I had him hid out in the woods." She rested the shotgun against the railing and hurried down the steps, stumbling on the bottom one where it had been damaged.

Polly came to a stop and stared at her father with wide, horrified eyes.

"Oh, my God," escaped her lips, barely audible.

"Help me get him into the house. Step back. I'll drive him closer. It's best if we don't touch him too much."

"The burns," she said, understanding the problem immediately. "Did Hawkins do this to him?"

"He did it to himself," Slocum said. He secured the buggy before gingerly lifting Neville and getting him started up the steps.

The injured man moved slowly, but he went under his own power, showing some life remained in him. His daughter fearfully reached out to him on the other side. He took her hand and let her help him the rest of the way to the top of the steps. Slocum opened the door. The two of them fell through, Polly unable to support her pa's weight on her own.

Before Slocum entered, he took a long, hard look at the road leading from the ranch house. Only when he felt certain no one had followed did he go in to help the woman with her father.

"His room's there. His and Ma's."

Slocum heard the catch in Polly's voice and knew what ran through her mind. Her ma was dead. Her pa would be soon enough, too.

"What happened to him?" she asked. "Did Hawkins do this?"

Slocum explained how Liam Neville had attacked the wedding using the explosive as he wrestled him through the door and laid him as gently as possible on the bed. Red stained the bedspread as Neville rolled about in pain.

"He's bleeding. We have to stop it. Boil some water and soak rags in it," Slocum said.

"You know what you're doing?"

Slocum did. He had tended wounds during the war, but seldom had he seen any as fierce as these burns. Mostly a man taking shrapnel either lost a limb or died. Somehow, Neville had survived wounds as bad as any sustained on the battlefield facing howitzers and minié balls specifically designed to kill.

Pulling out his knife, Slocum began slicing off the man's clothing and casting the bloody strips into a corner. By the time Polly returned with the hot water and clean bandages, Slocum had stripped off the shirt to reveal the worst of the wounds.

"Oh," Polly said. She began to wobble. Slocum caught her. "Sorry," she said. "I'm not usually this frail."

"Not that," Slocum said. "You've never seen wounds like this before."

"Is he going to make it, John?"

"He's a determined man."

That was all the answer he could give. If he had money to bet on the matter, no odds, no matter how great, could entice him to believe Liam Neville would be alive when the sun came up in the morning. He set to work, using the tip of his knife to worry out bits of wood from the man's body. It took some doing to keep the opened wounds from bleeding. Pressure and a bit of hot water sloshed on the wound helped.

He worked for the better part of an hour before realizing Neville weakened because of his crude doctoring. Slocum patched up what remained. The sight of the left side of his head completely smoothed off by the explosion turned his stomach. Slocum used the last of the bandages to cover the spot where the man's ear ought to have been, then wrapped a final turn around the head to hide the empty eye socket.

"He's asleep," Polly said in wonder. Slocum shared this astonishment. He knew his medical skills were limited. Neville should have died before now, yet he still drew ragged breaths and stirred feebly on the bed.

Slocum led her out of the room and pulled the door shut behind.

"Wait, no, I need to watch over him. I can't see or hear him if the door's shut."

Slocum let her push the door wide. As worried as she was, she'd jump at the slightest sound from the room, even if there wasn't anything she could do for him.

"Did he kill Hawkins?"

"I don't know. The dynamite did kill a passel of townspeople. How far he threw the dynamite before it exploded matters."

Slocum tried to re-create the scene in his head. The best he could remember, the dynamite hadn't gone very far from Neville's hand when it exploded. He had murdered dozens of innocent people but likely hadn't touched the man whose death he most sought.

"I didn't think he had the gumption to get to town. He was so weak after getting out of the coffin. I had him hidden away in the woods where Hawkins's men could never find him if they came looking." Polly shivered and hugged herself, in spite of the afternoon being so hot and sticky. "I never thought he would go after Hawkins like this."

"He knew where the undertaker would be and realized there might not be a better chance at killing him."

"Is that why you were there?" She stared hard at him and read the answer. "I'm glad you didn't kill Hawkins. If anyone does it, Pa ought to be the one after all that horrible man's done to this family."

"This attempt will drive Hawkins away. He'll disappear until Julian and his gang find your pa."

"I'm not turning my own father over to them. They'd kill him out of hand."

"I know," Slocum said softly. "It won't matter. A man like Hawkins isn't going to leave the town he has bought lock, stock, and barrel. Bullying folks pleases him as much as owning the land and herds. He'll poke his ugly head up eventually. When he does, I'll be there."

"I want Pa to be there beside you, John. He deserves his chance to get even."

"There's no getting even," Slocum said. "Even killing Hawkins isn't going to change things."

"It'll keep him from doing what he does to other people. He needs to be brought to heel. Killing him is the only way to do that."

Slocum agreed.

"You watch after him while I hide the buggy, in case anyone comes hunting."

It took him fifteen minutes to find a spot in the nearby woods to cover the buggy with fallen tree branches. He hobbled the horse to let it graze only yards away from a running stream. Slocum took his time returning to the house, expecting pursuit but not finding it. When he finally returned to the ranch house, he found Polly sitting upright on the sofa, asleep.

He settled down beside her. She murmured in her sleep, took his arm, and pulled him close, then lay her head on his shoulder. He put his arm around her and held her. Slocum intended to stay alert and watch for Julian and his gang, but he had been too keyed up for too long.

In a few minutes, his head tipped over and rested on hers. Both slept as if they were dead.

12

When Slocum opened his eyes, it was evening and already dark. He felt Polly stir and moved gently to be sure he didn't wake her. Polly muttered as he lowered her to the sofa, then she drew up her feet and remained asleep as he softly stepped away and went to see how her father fared.

Liam Neville lay flat on his back, his breathing harsh and labored. Slocum dripped some water on the man's cracked, burned lips. The sleeping man stirred but otherwise showed no sign of being alive. With a quick move, Slocum's hand flew to his six-shooter when he heard a noise at the bedroom door.

Silhouetted there stood Polly.

"You're looking after him just fine, John. Thank you."

"I wish I had been able to keep him from throwing the bomb. He wouldn't have killed half the town or ended up like this."

"Pa always was headstrong. Once he fixed on something, he was as fierce as any javelina. He'd take on any man twice his weight and strength."

"He'd usually win, unless I miss my guess," Slocum said.

"I'm the same way," Polly said.

"Headstrong?" Slocum had to smile.

Then the smile faded when he saw her shadow-cloaked figure strip off her blouse and hold it at arm's length a moment before dropping it. She turned to give him a profile. Her pert breasts were slightly upturned. She ran her hands over her sides and stopped under her boobs to pinch the nipples. Even in the dark, Slocum saw how they hardened. He felt himself responding with more than equal hardness.

She stepped back into the sitting room, working at her jeans as she moved. They came off like a snake molting. The denim second skin took a second to step free of, but when she turned back to him, she was entirely nude. Faint light from outside highlighted her curves, masked delightful valleys, and made her the most desirable woman he had ever seen.

"John." Her voice came low, husky, inviting.

Slocum stripped off his gun belt and quickly added his coat, vest, and shirt.

"Do you want help getting out of your jeans?"

"I can do it. I just want to look at you."

As he spoke, distant lightning flashed and illuminated her pale figure, turning her into a goddess carved in marble. As the light faded, Slocum moved faster to kick off his boots and strip off his pants. Another lightning bolt lit the room, giving both of them a new and different look.

Polly had reached down between her legs and stroked over her private parts. The lightning reflected off tiny drops of her inner oils now caught in the tangled mat of her bush. She caught her breath as the same light showed the erection at his groin.

They each took a step forward. Slocum reached out to touch her cheek. She turned her face and kissed his hand, but he moved it down to her throat to feel the pulse of her excitement. A soft sob escaped her lips when he stroked lower, down between her breasts. Not content only to appreciate the warmth and throbbing of her heart, he slid up a silky smooth mound to the nip capping it. He caught the rubbery tip and rolled it around between thumb and forefinger. Polly sagged a little and moved closer until he felt the heat from her body.

It was his turn to gasp as she reached down and grabbed hold of his manhood. She stroked along the length, then clamped down more firmly.

"It's like a pump handle," she said. "What happens if I begin to pump?"

"Prime the pump, let me do the pumping," he said.

Slocum closed his eyes as he felt her begin stroking up and down his length, then toy with the hairy sac tightening beneath.

"Prime it like this?"

She sank to her knees, robbing him of the delightful feel of her breasts. But he couldn't find the words to complain. Her lips circled the tip of his erection and took him into her mouth. The bulbous end stroked along the inside of her cheek before moving deeper into her throat. She swallowed, and he almost lost control.

Her hands circled his body and cupped his butt so she could pull him deeper into her mouth. Slocum opened his eyes and looked around. The room was illuminated by a distant lightning flash. Looking down to where he vanished into her mouth gave him a feeling of unreality, yet the way her tongue pressed against the underside of his organ was anything but illusion. As she sucked a little harder, her lips moving up and down, her teeth scoring his sensitive manhood, her tongue pushing and probing and trying to coax out his juices, he was excited to the point of no return.

"My turn," he said, pushing her away.

"No, I want more," she said in a sex-husky voice.

"You'll get it. After I drink my fill."

"What?"

He pushed her onto her back. She lay back, her knees

opening for him. He sank between her legs. The tangled mat between her legs was dotted with her inner juices. Dipping low, he scooped up one drop after another without actually touching her. When she protested, his tongue dragged the length of the pink curtains protecting her inner fastness. This sent a shudder through her body. Her legs rose on either side of his head. He drove his tongue forward, parted those delicate nether lips, and then plunged into her sex well.

She cried out. Her thighs clamped firmly on either side of his head. Deaf now, virtually blind, he had to rely on his sense of touch and taste. The salty fluids from her inner core drove him on. He lashed with his tongue, roughly touching her everywhere he could reach. From the tiny pink spire at the top of the V to the bottom, he didn't miss a spot. Polly thrashed about, moaning and crying out in excitement as he laved and licked and sucked.

Then her legs released his head. She propped herself up on her elbows and looked down at him. Her face had flushed. The red reached down to the tops of her tits.

"Enough, John, or not enough. I want more. I want *you*. In me. Now!"

He licked the length of her hidden slit, to her belly, and dipped low into her navel before working up to the canyon between her breasts. The oral assault robbed her of the strength even to hold herself up on her elbows.

Then she screamed in desire as his hips moved forward, and he sank balls deep in the cavity he had so recently probed with his tongue.

"Oh, yes, that's what I want."

"No," he said, "this is what you want."

He began stroking, slowly at first as he felt the warmth and tightness all around his length. She tensed around him, urging him to greater speed. He kept up the pace he wanted. It drove her crazy with lust. When she arched her back and jammed her crotch down around his hidden length, he knew his own control was slipping. He began pistoning faster. The heated tide built irresistible pressure in his loins. He stroked faster. The friction grew until he knew it was not possible for him to last any longer.

Arching his back, he thrust as far into her as possible. She rose to meet him, twisting from side to side to give even greater pleasure. Then he lost all control and spewed his seed into her hungry center.

She clawed at his shoulders as she pulled herself up and struggled to take him even deeper inside. Then they sank back to the floor, exhausted from their passionate efforts.

Slocum looked down into her dewy eyes. She rose up enough to give him a quick kiss before dropping back.

"You wore me out."

"I was inspired." He rotated his hips a little, but he was already limp within her. Slocum slipped free and rolled to lie beside her. "It must have been the storm."

Rain pelted the roof now. The thunder came only seconds after every lightning bolt.

"It's warm."

He moved his hand down between their legs and cupped her privates.

"It is."

She giggled like a schoolgirl and snuggled closer, safe within the circle of his arms.

Slocum slipped to sleep about the same time she did.

When he awoke the next morning, he was alone on the floor with a blanket tossed over his hips. He pushed the blanket away. The new day's heat was already building and made it too much.

"You should cover up. It's not proper to go around naked like that," she said. "Come on and eat. After you get dressed."

"You didn't mind last night."

"You distracted me."

"But I don't now?" He looked down at his groin. "I reckon not."

This brought a laugh to her lips. Slocum fetched his clothes and dressed. After he strapped on his six-gun, he wondered if life could get better. Then he heard Liam Neville moaning from the other room. That caused a flood of unpleasant memories.

"I just checked him. He's not looking too good," Polly said. "Isn't there anything more we can do for him?"

"No doctor could do more. Whiskey might cut through the pain." Even as he spoke, he wondered if that was true. Drinking the whiskey himself or giving it to Polly would be a better use.

"I know. Here. Eat." She pushed a plate of ham and fried eggs toward him. "Only got a couple chickens left. And that's the last of the hog."

Slocum shoveled in the food. It settled into his belly and renewed his strength. It had been too long since he'd eaten this well. Or was it the food and the long night with Polly that made him feel so confident now?

As he finished, he pushed the plate back and hooked his thumbs in his gun belt.

"Mighty good," he said.

"You're thinking of something else. What is it, John?"

"We can't keep your pa here. Hawkins will have his men searching everywhere for him."

"They recognized him? You said the attack was quick and—"

"Somebody will know him. The townspeople will be as eager to string him up as Hawkins is to bury him again."

This made Polly shudder. She glanced in the direction of the bedroom, then down to her plate. Slocum knew where her thoughts strayed. Fighting Leonard Hawkins had turned her father into a killer hunted by everyone in Espero.

"We should leave, shouldn't we, John? I mean go as far as possible." She looked up. Her eyes blazed. "I won't do it. That means Hawkins wins. I'd rather die than let that son of a bitch win!"

"I'm not going to give up," Slocum said. "I have my own reasons, but then you know that. You and your brother dug me up."

"Where can I take him so we can keep fighting?"

Slocum wasn't sure who she meant by "we," but he wasn't going to ask. He had to find Hawkins. If the man had died in the explosion, good. Slocum would feel robbed, but the undertaker would have been brought to justice for his crimes.

"You take your pa to where you thought he was safe before."

"I can't. That's still on our property. Anyone looking will find that shed." She thought a moment, then said, "I know a place south of here, down by the river. I can sketch a map for you." She eagerly pushed her plate aside and dipped her finger in the coffee to draw on the tablecloth. Slocum reached across and grabbed her wrist.

"It's better if I don't know. What I don't know I can't spill."

"And I won't know where you are either," she said with a note of sadness. "We should get out of here right away, shouldn't we?"

"Last night would have been better."

"Last night could never have been better." She leaned across the table and gave him a quick peck on the cheek. "It can be that good again. Maybe better?"

"I'll fetch the buggy unless you have some way of carrying your pa that's better."

"I have my horse. We'd have to ride double, and I'm not sure I could hold him the whole way."

Slocum left the house and hitched up the horse to the buggy. He didn't like asking Polly for her horse, but he had to be more mobile than staying on foot. Driving the buggy around to the front, he pulled up. To his surprise, Polly was already helping her pa down the steps. Liam Neville wasn't helping much, but he managed to keep from putting his entire weight on her. He looked up, recognized Slocum, and made a gesture with his hand. This exhausted him.

Slocum got Neville into the buggy, where he sagged.

He turned to Polly, who looked on anxiously.

"He's going to be all right, isn't he?"

He kissed her hard. For a moment, she resisted, her thoughts still on her father. Then she melted into his arms and returned the kiss.

"Everything's going to be fine," Slocum said. He hoped he wasn't lying to her.

She smiled weakly, then climbed in, snapped the reins, and got the horse pulling. As she left the yard, she yelled over her shoulder, "My horse is out back. Her name's Buttermilk!"

Slocum let the buggy rattle out of sight, then swept through the house to get what supplies would serve him best. When he found Polly's horse, he almost despaired. It was a swaybacked mare that hadn't seen better days in a year. It was all he had, though, so he slung his supplies over the horse's rump and stepped up. The horse didn't buckle under his weight. That was a good sign, but he doubted it could run.

He trotted it around the ranch house a few times, then let the horse gallop. He slowed quickly to prevent tiring out the old nag. While not as sturdy as the pinto he'd left in Espero when he had pulled Neville from the barn, it would do.

Immediately on starting down the road he heard shouts and catcalls from ahead. The thick trees along this part of the road warned him the riders were too close for comfort. He steered the reluctant horse into the thicket, then waited, hoping the gum tree proved enough of a camouflage to let him go unnoticed.

The riders passed within a dozen yards. He kept his hand on the mare's neck to quiet her. The first half-dozen men he didn't recognize, but the two trailing riders were from Julian's gang. A posse had been sent out with the outlaws a part of it, to report back anything discovered.

"This is their place. I say we burn it to the ground."

"Neville might be inside," protested another.

"Then we sift through the ashes to find him."

This met with a round of cheers. Slocum waited for them to disappear around a bend in the road. The prudent thing was for him to ride away as fast as he could without being discovered. That was prudent. He unfastened the rope at his knee, spun it out into a lasso, then let the loop fall quiet beside his knee.

Making his way through the thicket proved tedious, and he and the horse picked up more stickers and burrs than he could shake a stick at, but he finally got to the road so he could trail Julian's men.

His pace was fast enough that he overtook them before they reached the ranch house. With a deft twist of his roping hand, he got the lasso spinning and cast it as the trailing man saw what was in store for him. A loud yelp was quickly followed by a thud as Slocum let the running noose come down around his shoulders so he could drag him to the ground. He charged forward as the man struggled on the ground. His partner stared in disbelief, giving Slocum the element of surprise.

He drew his six-shooter, leaned far out, and swung. The barrel caught the man on the cheek. He recoiled, spooking his horse. In a heartbeat the man flew from his horse and landed hard. Slocum grabbed the horse's reins and savagely jerked down to keep it from pawing at the air. As he brought Polly's horse around, he leveled his pistol.

With the pair on the ground a few yards apart, Slocum aimed at a spot midway between them.

"If you want to go on sucking air, tell me if Leonard Hawkins is still alive."

From the smirks on both men's faces, he had his answer.

"Where's Julian? Where's your camp?"

"No, don't tell him, Abner," cautioned the one Slocum had buffaloed. He never hesitated. He fired. The slug took the man high in the chest, knocking him flat onto the ground.

Slocum swung his six-shooter around.

"Tell me, Abner. Fast."

"H-He . . . We got a camp right behind the funeral parlor. Mr. Hawkins, he wanted us close by if anybody in the town got too belligerent. That's his word, belligerent."

The shot had attracted attention from the posse, but they didn't know what to make of it since a second shot hadn't alerted them to any kind of a fight.

"Toss me the end of the rope."

Abner started to shake himself free of the loop, but Slocum was too quick for him. He rode forward and snatched the end from the man's hands. Trailing the other outlaw's horse, Slocum commenced to dragging Abner along the rough double-rutted road. The man yelled for a dozen yards, then stopped. Slocum suspected he had hit his head on a rock. He threw down the end of the rope, trotted forward, and caught the reins of Abner's horse.

With the two outlaws' horses in addition to Polly's, he could ride all day if necessary.

But all he had to do was return to town. He knew where Julian and his gang were. And he knew where Hawkins was.

As he rode, he plotted their deaths.

13

Slocum took his time riding back to Espero, waiting for the shadows to lengthen so he could escape any sentinels Julian might have posted along the road. When he reached the outskirts, dusk hid his features. Not riding the same horse and having two others trotting behind might also provide some cover, but Slocum doubted that. Anyone Julian—or Hawkins—posted would be smart enough to recognize him. With the countryside filled with posses hunting down Liam Neville, it was a stretch of the imagination to believe they didn't also look for him.

At the edge of town he heard the mournful peals from the huge bell Hawkins had put into a ten-foot-tall bell tower in front of his funeral parlor. A solemn note sounded every thirty seconds. Slocum counted, then nodded an instant before a new peal rolled out over the town.

He wanted to investigate, but another matter occupied him first. He rode to the livery stable. The barn Neville had blown to smithereens still smoldered some distance away. He expected to see corpses stacked like cordwood but nothing of the sort showed through the twilight. Sniffing, he tried to catch any hint of decomposing bodies. All that made his nose wrinkle were the mingled odors of burned wood and the sharp ammonia scent of detonated dynamite.

Dismounting, he led his horses into the livery stable. The owner snored peacefully in a back stall. Slocum looked into every stall until he found his horse and gear. Only then did he awaken the man and dicker some for the return of his own property and the sale of the three horses in his possession. Selling Polly's horse bothered him but only for a moment. Chances were good she wouldn't need it if her pa died—and Slocum doubted the man would survive to see another day. She would have the buggy and horse to ride in style to Dexter Junction. Selling them there would get her money for a railroad ticket out of Texas.

And if he lived, Liam Neville would require almost constant attention. Polly had no place to go in the buggy in that case nor would she miss her horse.

The thought crossed his mind he could always give her the money he got from selling Buttermilk. That gave him a good reason to seek her out again. She was fiery and the kind of woman he appreciated most in life—and in bed. If she moved on after her pa died, Slocum saw no reason the two of them couldn't ride together.

For a woman like Polly Neville, remaining on the Box N would be nothing but a constant reminder of bad days and worse people in Espero.

He pocketed seventy-five dollars for the three horses and another hundred for the gear. So much money stuffed into his vest pocket almost compensated for having Julian and his men rob him.

It would take far more than getting back the money they stole to leaven his desire for revenge. Awakening in the coffin the way he had would burn in his soul forever.

Best of all, he got back his own horse and rifle. He didn't remember where he had dropped it when he had lit out to stop Neville, but it had to have been close by his horse for someone to stuff it back into the saddle sheath. A quick check convinced him it wasn't damaged and would stand him in good stead when he had to use it again.

After he left the livery stables richer and feeling better about his chances of settling the score with Hawkins, he noticed the funeral bell still tolled. Counting under his breath brought him to thirty seconds and another clang. He knew better, but he had to see what was going on. He rode around back of the mortuary and saw where Julian and his men were camped.

Three cooking fires warned him the gang leader had recruited more men than he could handle alone. As much as he wanted Julian and the men who had buried him to end up in graves of their own, he would forgo that pleasure in return for putting a bullet into Hawkins's fat gut. He was the source of all the trouble in town and in Slocum's life.

Slocum had dealt with such men before. All the way from Bloody Bill Anderson and William Quantrill on, after the war had been filled with men itching to do harm—and every one of them had come to a grievous end because of John Slocum. He took no real pleasure in killing, but for Leonard Hawkins, he would make an exception.

He looked up in alarm when the bell did not deliver its usual peal at the thirty-second interval. The men in Julian's camp stirred but made no sign they considered the cessation out of the ordinary. Slocum rode around to the street in front of the funeral parlor in time to see Miranda wiping her hands on a cloth, then mopping her face. The oppressive heat hadn't slackened as the sun went down. If she had been ringing the bell for long, the exertion would have explained the way she turned back to the mortuary, shoulders bent and step hesitant.

Slocum found a spot down the street to tether his horse. He returned to peer in the mortuary's open front door. What breeze there was stirred about in the vestibule but hardly moved the heavy velvet curtains hiding the viewing room.

He stepped back when he heard a soft swishing sound. A cloud of dust flew from inside, the product of Miranda's aggressive sweeping. She didn't look up until he softly called her name.

"What?" Then her eyes went wide when she saw him. "Oh, no, you can't be here!"

He stepped into the vestibule and pressed his back against the wall. It was still warm from the day in the sun. Like a striking snake, he reached for her and caught her wrist. He pulled her close until their bodies touched.

"So you're married." Slocum held up her left hand with the large diamond ring on the fourth finger. "How's married life so far?"

"Don't be like that, John. Please."

"You want to thank me for not killing him before you got hitched?"

The question caused her eyes to grow wide. She started to speak, but no words came out. After a strangled gurgle, she swallowed hard and then said, "Thank you. Now you can do me another favor and get the hell away from me!"

"I'll be happy to do so," he said, "after I kill Hawkins." He watched her reaction. Before, she had begged him to let her groom live. Now she made no protest.

"That won't be necessary."

"You wouldn't mind if I put six slugs into his rotten heart?"

"There's no need for you to waste the ammo."

"That's a strange thing to say."

"Leonard is not a well man. He . . . he is prone to seizures and one will kill him someday soon."

"That's the first I've heard of any malady other than his gout."

"John, you must go before he finds you—before Julian or one of his men spots you. I don't want anything to happen to you."

"Thanks," he said with only a touch of sarcasm. "Not

only do you value my hide now, you don't want me wasting my ammunition."

"If you stay and meddle in my affairs, you'll end up getting hurt. Or worse."

"By Hawkins? Or the man who followed you here from Dexter Junction?" Again he had rattled her, but Miranda covered her surprise.

"You're nothing but a meddling cowboy who doesn't know when he has it good."

"I had it good. I had a wad of greenbacks stuffed into my pocket for escorting you here, but they got taken off me before Julian buried me alive."

"Is that all? The money?" She pushed away from him and wrenched her left hand free of his grasp. "I'll get you the money. How much? Four hundred? Five hundred? I'll give you five hundred to ride from Espero and never look back."

"That's mighty tempting. You'd give me so much money? You who Hawkins has sweeping up like a maid and ringing the bell outside? What was that about?"

"The bell? I had to ring it ten times for each death at the wedding. Leonard is going to be busy for a week interring the thirty-two that died."

"How did you and him escape such an explosion?"

Slocum pressed his ear against the wall, listening for movement anywhere in the mortuary. All he heard was the creak and groan of a building settling. Being so near the heart of Hawkins's power made him edgy.

"I don't know. We were up front. I never saw the man with the dynamite. The parson had just pronounced us man and wife and Leonard had put the ring on my finger. It didn't fit. It hurt, so I jerked back and lost my balance. I fell down as the explosion ripped through the barn."

"How'd Hawkins get away?"

"I asked. He said he saw the crazy man and dived down behind the dais. He was so angry at ruining his suit."

Slocum stared at her. She spoke of Hawkins as if he were a stranger, someone who meant nothing to her.

"He didn't try to save you?"

"No." For the first time, hardness came into her tone. Her jaw tensed. She turned away so he couldn't see her as clearly in the faint light.

"He doesn't love you. Do you love him?"

"I married him, didn't I?"

"That's no answer," Slocum said.

Before he could press her, he heard voices from deeper inside the funeral home.

"That's Hawkins. I have to fix him dinner." Miranda bit her lower lip, then said with forced sincerity, "I must go fix *Leonard's* supper." She laid her hand on his arm. "Be careful, John. Whatever there is between you two, ignore it. Leave. Leonard will be just fine."

"The money," Slocum said harshly. "Give me the money he owes me."

"Oh, well, yes, of course." She sounded disappointed, as if she expected more from him. It wasn't what Slocum intended, but he wanted an excuse to stay around until he could get the undertaker in his sights.

The voices grew louder. Slocum recognized Hawkins and Julian. He reached for his six-gun, but Miranda stopped him. She silently shook her head, then put a finger to her lips to keep him quiet. Then she held up four fingers.

"Guards?"

She nodded vigorously and pushed him toward the front door and into the night.

Just as Slocum slipped through, he caught himself and waited just beyond the door.

"There you are, Miranda. You miscounted on the bells. You were two rings short. Which Espero citizen did you disrespect by your inattention?"

"Why, Leonard, uh, I thought I counted properly. There

wasn't anyone I intended to insult. Their family, I mean, since they are dead and don't care."

"Don't say that. I like to think—I *know*—they are watching from above. You will never get into Heaven by heaping such dishonor on all the deceased."

"But, dear, you said I only missed two—that means one of those who died. I—"

"You will fix my dinner, then go and start over. Two tolls, thirty seconds apart for each of the deceased."

"That's more than another half hour of ringing the bell. Won't the rest of the town protest ruining their sleep? Can't I do it tomorrow morning before the burials? This is only our second night together, dearest."

Slocum slipped his six-shooter free. The sound of Miranda being slapped set his blood to boiling. Only luck saved him from foolishly going to her rescue. His coat caught on a nail in the wall, preventing him from whirling about. At the instant he would have confronted Hawkins, three of Julian's gang stepped out to look around.

The night hid Slocum as the men looked into the street but not behind them against the wall where he was caught. They made a few crude comments about what a night with Miranda would be like, then went back inside and closed the door. A locking bar dropped into place, making it impossible for Slocum to pursue them even if he had wanted to. He gently unhooked the thread from the nail head, then walked to the side of the building and looked back toward the outlaw camp.

Too many of Julian's gang sat around their cooking fires for him to have any hope of taking them out one by one. Slocum stepped back, looked up to the funeral parlor roof, and went to the water barrel under the gutter. He climbed to the rim of the barrel, gripped the downspout, and pulled himself up. The nails holding the drainpipe pulled free with a mournful creak, but before Slocum found himself falling, he pulled himself up over the gutter and onto the sloping roof. He waited a few minutes, listening for any hint that he had been seen.

He looked over the gang's camp. Seeing nothing to show they were aware of his presence, Slocum made his way along the roof to the chimney and began prying loose a few bricks next to it. When he got his spyhole clear, he flopped belly down and put his eye to the opening. He made sense out of what he saw in the room below. A table was set with a meal, untouched. Muffled voices came from another room. He changed his perspective, then caught his breath.

Moving like a ghost to the table, the mystery man stopped, took something from his pocket, and poured a powder over the food on one plate. He looked up suddenly, then rushed out of Slocum's sight as Hawkins and Miranda appeared in the room and sat at the table.

The food that had been dusted sat in front of Hawkins.

Slocum tried to pry a larger hole to get a better view, but to do so would create too much noise. He shifted again, trying to see Miranda. She sat with her back to him. From the way she leaned forward slightly, it was as if she was intensely interested in whatever Hawkins said—or she waited for him to fork in food from his plate.

Every time the undertaker lifted the fork with a morsel impaled on it, he hesitated, then lowered it back to his plate. Slocum wished he could hear what was being said, but both spoke in low tones.

"Now," Hawkins said loudly, throwing his fork onto his plate with a loud clatter. He stood. "The time is now!"

"Must we, my dear?" Miranda stirred uneasily. "Let's finish supper so we will have energy for . . . the entire night."

"Now."

Hawkins shoved his chair back and came around the table, grabbing Miranda by the arm and jerking her to her feet.

"Now."

"But, Leonard—"

He kissed her with a savage passion that caused Slocum to wonder if he could get a good shot through his peephole. Then any hope of plugging Hawkins disappeared with the couple below.

Slocum made his way to the edge of the roof, intending to jump down and find a window. Treating Miranda the way Hawkins had infuriated him, but on a colder, deadlier level he knew this was his best chance of getting his revenge on the undertaker. Before he could drop to the ground, Hawkins and Miranda came around the building and took a path leading away from the funeral parlor. Slocum slid his six-gun from the holster but never had a clear shot. The dark complicated his shot, but Hawkins pulled Miranda along behind him, using her as an unintentional shield.

Slocum stood and saw that the path led into the woods some distance away. From the way Miranda protested, he wondered if she had second thoughts about not letting him kill Hawkins before the marriage.

The couple disappeared into the woods. All Slocum saw were the occasional flashes of lightning bugs. He looked at the sky. Tonight was clear with no hint of a summer storm.

A grim smile crossed his lips. The storm would be wherever Hawkins took the unwilling woman.

He crouched when he heard someone prowling about under him. Carefully looking over the gutter, he saw a dark figure move around, then kneel and look at the soft earth hunting for tracks. When the man found the path taken by Hawkins and Miranda, he set out after them.

Slocum followed the man with his sights centered on his back, then lowered his pistol. If anyone saved Miranda this night, let it be her mysterious companion. Something else piqued Slocum's curiosity.

When the man vanished into the woods, Slocum gripped the gutter, fell forward, and slammed into the wall, hanging for a second before dropping to the ground. He made some noise but not enough to alert any of Hawkins's guards. With his step silent, he bent low and moved as easily as any Apache to find the door where the trio had left the funeral parlor. A quick twist of the knob opened the door, letting Slocum enter.

The interior proved darker than outside. Without the stars overhead to give some light and no oil lamp burning, Slocum had to edge carefully through the room. He bumped into a coffin and recoiled. Using a lucifer from the tin he carried in his vest pocket, he got a good look at the woman in the casket. Holding the flaring match higher, he looked around the room. It was crowded with coffins. Hawkins was the only undertaker in town and must have worked overtime to prepare so many bodies for burial this fast.

Before the match burned down to his fingers, he hurried through the maze of coffins to the door leading into the vestibule. From here he made his way through to the viewing room and, using his nose to follow the smell of cooked food, found the living quarters in a rear room. The small kitchen opened onto the dining room Slocum had spied on.

He stood in the doorway and studied the room. Over beside the chimney a tall cabinet stood half open. This had to be where Miranda's companion had hidden. The firelight kept it hidden in shadows while illuminating the rest of the room with a soft light.

Slocum went to the table. Miranda wasn't much of a cook from the look of the food, but it was better than anything he could have whipped up on the trail. He reached for a slice of beef on her plate, smeared some gravy on it, and started to sample it. He froze when he saw a rat on the table sniffing about.

The rat went to Hawkins's plate. Its whiskers wiggled about as it made a small meal from the food. Then it went into convulsions, flopped onto its side, kicked tiny clawed feet in the air, and died.

Slocum dropped the beef. He had seen the mystery man pour powder on Hawkins's food. He might have similarly treated Miranda's.

He left without touching anything else. Miranda might be in as much danger from her stalker as she was from her new husband.

14

Slocum cautiously stepped away from the funeral parlor, then froze when he heard two men joking with each other—and coming toward him from the direction of Julian's camp. The only spot he could see to take cover was in a shallow ditch. He eased himself down into the muck and lay quietly as the men trod along the path he had intended to follow.

"The boss said to escort them back when they was done."

"With a woman what looks like her, I'd be all night and half into tomorrow."

"Oh, yeah, you? You'd be done in ten seconds. What'd you do the rest of the night? Play checkers?"

"I'd jump her bones, that's for sure."

"Not her bones I want. Did you see the hitch in her git-along when she walked on up to the altar? That warn't no bustle under her wedding dress. That was the real thing."

The two went to the woods but did not enter as Hawkins, Miranda, and her stalker had. They positioned themselves on either side of the trail, settling down and shutting up a few yards apart. After a few minutes, Slocum spied a tiny orange coal glowing in the night. One had built himself a smoke. It was close to five minutes before the cigarette smoke reached where Slocum lay, still wary of others joining the two guards. The still night became increasingly oppressive with its heat and heavy air.

Realizing he had to move, Slocum began inching backward in the ditch. Mud sucked obscenely as he pried himself loose. The sounds were muffled by his body and never reached the two guards at the edge of the woods. He got to the dry patch around the funeral home and then pressed his back against the wall, alert for anyone from Julian's camp spotting him. Only when he was satisfied that he was not seen did he stand and walk slowly to the front and then down the street to where he had left his horse.

Too much had gone on for him to make sense of it. All he knew was that Leonard Hawkins had robbed him and then had him buried alive. Whether Hawkins had had his hand on the spade shoveling the dirt onto the coffin or he'd left that to his henchmen didn't matter. He had to pay for that and so much more to the people in and around Espero.

Slocum had never seen himself as a crusader. Let the law handle what it could, but Hawkins had done more than could ever be punished by even a noose. He took the reins and walked his horse rather than riding to keep from getting mud all over his saddle. The horse looked at him sideways, grateful not to be drenched by the river of muck Slocum shed as he walked along.

Julian still hunted for him and the Nevilles. With Polly and her pa safely hidden somewhere far away, that meant a few of the gang would be occupied for a good, long time on a fruitless search. Whatever reduced the number of guns he faced suited Slocum. Too many for him to fight openly remained camped. He had to figure out a way to get to Hawkins in spite of his bodyguards. In his present condition, Slocum was distracted by itchy clothing and bugs that wanted to dine on his flesh.

He found a bathhouse and broke in. Slocum started water

heating on a stove and stripped off his clothes. It took the better part of an hour for him to get clean, then wash his clothing in the bathwater. He wrung out his clothing and put it close to the hot stove to dry. In the humid air it took forever before the jeans were dry enough to put on, but Slocum wasn't in any hurry. Sitting naked beside the stove, thinking hard about what to do, let his tensed muscles relax.

By the time he dressed and had dropped a silver dollar on the stool next to the galvanized bathtub, the sun was poking up over the rolling hills to the east. It was going to be another sultry day. And from the ringing bell, one that would be longer than usual for many of the town's residents.

Slocum watched a steady stream of men and women dressed in mourning clothes make their way toward Hawkins's funeral parlor. He joined the procession, trying to blend in. He felt as if he stood out like a sore thumb, but cleaning the mud off had given him that small amount of camouflage. Everyone around him wore stored clothing that smelled of cedar to keep the moths away. The people wore more than their Sunday finery on this day of mourning.

The women wore widow's weeds, and the men trudged along in solemn silence.

Slocum stopped when the knot of people around him did. He stared. A steady procession of wagons rattled from the funeral parlor along the road leading to the town cemetery. As he waited, he saw six wagons. Each one carried a small banner with the name of the deceased. As people identified their loved ones, they broke off from the crowd and walked beside the casket-laden wagon.

How Hawkins had rustled up so many wagons and had hammered together so many coffins in such a short time would have shown devotion to his trade. For Slocum it seemed more like an eagerness to put people six feet under.

He edged forward, then slipped off to the mortuary as Miranda came out the front door, looking haggard and defeated. What her first two nights as a married woman had been like wasn't something Slocum wanted to think on too long. She went to the bell cord on the tower between the funeral parlor and the street and began tolling slowly, not doing the measured one ring every thirty seconds she had the day before. This was a general calling to service, not an honor for each of the dead.

He waved to catch her eye, but she kept her eyes downcast. Seldom had Slocum seen a woman so beaten in spirit. Hawkins had done it in only a few days after meeting her for the first time.

Search the crowd as he might, Slocum couldn't locate the woman's stalker. He wanted to ask about the poison in the food, but there was no chance. From her look, Miranda hadn't eaten breakfast. If she stayed away from meals until Slocum stopped the man, she would be all right. And he couldn't have cared less if Hawkins gobbled up everything on the plate. As much as he wanted the satisfaction of taking out Hawkins himself, if another did it, he wasn't going to complain overly.

One wagon returned from the cemetery. Slocum watched as four of Julian's men hefted another coffin and loaded it into the wagon, complaining as they did so. Robbing banks was more to their liking than physical labor. One opined how he enjoyed that because it felt good shooting people and getting paid for it.

Slocum had shot his share of men during the war and after, and he had never cottoned much to it. For Leonard Hawkins, he would make an exception, and that was more like cleansing the world of a terrible canker. He wasn't going to enjoy the killing for the sake of taking another man's life.

But the notion of robbing a bank . . .

He had done his share of that, too, mostly to get money to eat. Guilt never intruded when he did something illegal. If it had, he would be cowering in a corner, gibbering like a fool. Life had been harsh, and he met it on its own terms. So far he had won, though he knew someday death would lay down the royal flush and beat any possible hand he might hold. This wasn't that day, and Hawkins had to be removed before he gave in to death.

Besides, memories of Polly kept poking into his head. She knew just the right things to say and do to keep him interested in living to see another dawn. While he intended to kill Hawkins for his own revenge, the undertaker's death would give the woman some relief. It might even be enough to soothe the powerful hurt her pa had taken unto himself trying to kill Hawkins. Slocum wished he could have stopped the elder Neville from killing so many of his fellow townspeople, but the way Neville acted showed he had gone plumb loco. When he recovered from his wounds, he might never be right in the head again. The deaths of his wife and son were part of that, but being buried alive beside his precious Marie might be enough to keep him out of his head until the day he died.

Slocum reflected on how different people dealt with grief. Those around him watching the coffin-filled wagons roll to the cemetery were proof. Some openly wept, both men and women. Others had a haggard, drawn expression. A small number had hardened emotionally to the world and its pitiless ways. Slocum wasn't sure which was best. All he knew was that shedding tears had been impossible for him over the years.

Getting even provided the most comfort.

Approaching Miranda as she bent her back into ringing the bell to mark the passing of so many people would gain him nothing but trouble. Too many of Julian's men milled about, some working to load coffins, others driving the wagons. From inside the funeral parlor came sawing and hammering sounds as more coffins were hastily built.

As he edged forward with a small segment of the crowd, he drifted farther to the edge until he finally stood by the ditch where he had taken refuge the night before. No sign of guards at the edge of the woods sent his heart pounding.

He walked slowly and purposefully along the muddy track to the spot where he had seen the one bodyguard smoking the night before. Traces of gray ash on a leaf of a tall butterfly bush showed where the smoker had carelessly flicked his cigarette. Mingled with the purple petals from the bush that had fallen to the ground Slocum saw a piece of unburnt rolling paper.

He pushed deeper into woods, following the trail. How many boots had trod this path before him, he couldn't tell, but grasses tried to overgrow the trail, telling him it wasn't as frequently traveled as it had been in the past. Pushing low-hanging branches away, he kept walking until he came to a muddy spot devoid of all weeds and grass, where many feet had recently trampled. He couldn't help staring at the white marble structure, almost five feet tall and as wide, that had been built so that the trees sheltered it from casual discovery.

On closer investigation he saw this was only the top of a set of marble steps going down fully ten feet. Shoulders brushing against the walls on either side of the staircase, he descended and found a teakwood door standing partially open. He used the toe of his boot to push the door open as he drew his six-shooter. The interior yielded up only absolute darkness. Using senses other than his eyes, he listened hard and heard nothing inside. The odors coming from the chamber made his nose wrinkle. He might have blundered into a brothel.

Edging forward, he saw a kerosene lamp on a low table just inside the door. Laying his six-gun on the table, he pulled the chimney off to expose the wick. He used a lucifer to light the lamp, replaced the glass mantle, and adjusted the light so a soft yellow glow filled the small chamber. He quickly snatched up his six-shooter when movement at the edge of his vision warned him.

Slocum relaxed a mite. He was too keyed up. He had been reduced to jumping at shadows. Worse than that, it was his own shadow cast across a section of strangely decorated wall. He began his investigation of the room, starting with the most obvious feature.

In the middle of the eight-by-ten room was a bed barely wide enough for two people.

"I doubt you enjoyed lying here in spite of the finery, Miranda," Slocum said softly, touching the rumpled, stained sheets. They were finely woven, expensive, almost like butter flowing under his fingers. The image of Hawkins on top of Miranda pumping away caused Slocum to pull back.

As he did, he looked around and saw the frescoes on the walls that had startled him earlier. He took a closer look at the figures. An artist had worked long hours creating the scene that circled the room. Slocum had seen a book of mythology once and recognized some of the creatures and their erotic tendencies, but others damned near made him blush. It took him some time to circle the room and return to the doorway. He tried to imagine what it had been like, in a fine bed with Miranda Madison, looking at the raunchy pictures as he made love to her. His imagination failed. Why would any man need more than the beautiful raven-haired woman in his arms?

Slocum backed away, then frowned when he saw how the bed had been constructed. It bore a striking resemblance to an oversized coffin. A cold shiver ran up and down his spine. He extinguished the lamp and hurried up the steps into the close, hot forest air. Being in the crypt had brought back terrible memories of being buried alive.

If anything, seeing Hawkins's love nest hardened his determination to put the undertaker six feet under. Slocum would even consider sealing the undertaker in his love vault, as long as he never escaped. Somehow that notion appealed to Slocum, just a little. Then he realized Hawkins would enjoy the paintings until the light burned out. He gave up on this idea because it allowed Hawkins a tiny bit of enjoyment before the suffocating death in the dark.

He started back toward the funeral parlor, then saw

another branching path that had been used recently. He looked around, saw no hint that Julian or his men patrolled the area, then set off to explore. The path curled into the deepest part of the woods. Trees here grew only a few feet apart, and off the path bramble bushes grew so thick that getting through them would require a big knife like Slocum had seen a Mexican carrying when he had drifted into Sonora. A machete, the man had called it. He used it to cut up dogs and threaten men afraid of big knives.

Slocum had never been afraid of a knife, no matter the size. He wished he had picked up the machete after his fight with the arrogant fool. It would have been useful now.

He came to a small clearing where another crypt had been built. The one appeared to be above ground and not sunk ten feet into the ground like Hawkins's love nest. Slocum circled and found only one door into the crypt. He turned to go when he saw a double rut leading to the door as if someone had been dragged inside.

Considering the heavy summer rains, whoever had been put into the crypt had been laid to rest recently. The heavy toll Liam Neville had taken among the townspeople trying to blow up Hawkins made an interment distressingly ordinary. But who deserved such a fancy sepulcher? Slocum examined the exterior but found no name chiseled anywhere. And why did it look as if someone had been dragged inside rather than carried in?

Slocum went cold inside. Hawkins had buried someone else alive. It might have been a fancy marble vault but above ground or below made no difference. The dark. The suffocation.

He tugged on the door, but it refused to open. Slocum looked around and found a sturdy limb that had fallen off a lightning-struck tree nearby. Wedging the end into a small crack, he applied increasing pressure until he thought his back would break. The memory of the grave added strength and determination to his assault on the door.

Inch by inch the door opened until Slocum got his fingers around the edge and gave a huge pull. He stumbled back, recovered, and returned to peer inside the crypt. Sunlight penetrated only a foot or so. Slocum struck another lucifer and held it up as it flared.

He felt as if he had stepped off a cliff and plunged downward.

Crucified on the back wall hung Liam Neville.

15

Slocum stepped closer and saw that blood had leaked from the nail holes in Neville's hands onto the stone floor. Other blood had dripped down the wall after Neville had smashed his head there repeatedly in pain. He made his way around the small room, his gut churning. Neville had been alive when he had been nailed up.

"Polly," he muttered under his breath.

Prowling about, he found partial bloody boot prints. The men who had done this to Neville had stood around a spell and watched him die. Slocum knelt and looked more closely at the footprints. If his gut had churned before, it tumbled over and over now. Two sets of footprints were larger than the third. The smallest prints might have been from a woman's boots.

Polly.

Julian and his gunmen had brought Neville's daughter here to watch him die a lingering death. No torture was beyond Hawkins and his henchmen. But what had they done with Polly? Slocum failed to find her tracks leaving the vault.

He went outside and studied the ground. He found more

boot prints now that he hunted for them off the trail. Grass had been crushed down but now sprang back. They had walked around the crypt within the past eight hours, but that told him nothing. Where had they gone? How had they found her and her father?

On hands and knees, Slocum used the sun angling through the trees to find even fainter traces. He crawled along, hoping to get a definite direction. He lost the trail, found it again as it went deeper into the woods until he lost the faint impressions entirely in the vegetation on the soft forest floor.

He wiped his hands off on his pants. Reaching for his Colt Navy and slipping because of mud might spell his death. Without a definite path to follow, Slocum crashed through the undergrowth, ignoring the sharp spines and nettles. He slowed his pace, then hunted around for a game trail or other way through the trees. No sign of anyone other than himself bulling through the undergrowth convinced him he was reacting emotionally and not methodically. When he came across another trail, he found one clear set of tracks.

He made the best time he could while keeping a sharp eye out for a possible ambush. But the single set of tracks went both ways. Polly had not been carried along this way as a prisoner, but it was all Slocum had to work on.

Another entryway to an underground crypt showed through the weeds. This structure was intentionally hidden. Slocum pushed back the foliage and went down the stone steps. A new padlock held the door shut. He pressed his ear against the wood panel to listen for any cries inside. Slocum realized Polly might not know help had come. He used the butt of his pistol to rap loudly several times.

"Polly, you in there? It's me, Slocum. Make a noise if you're inside."

He listened harder. Silence. Quiet as a tomb. He stepped back, ready to shoot off the lock, when he heard shouts from the woods. Backing off, going up the steps, he knelt and peered through the weeds and waited.

Two men armed with rifles came closer to the steps, but they didn't see him. He sighted on one and calculated his chances of taking him out first, then shooting the other before he realized they were under attack. Slocum eased back on the trigger, then released pressure when two more armed men joined the first pair.

"I don't know how she got away. Julian's gonna skin us alive if we don't find her."

"I tole you we oughta have nailed her up like we done her old man," said a grizzled man. His mouth sparkled when he spoke. The sun caught a gold tooth in the front of his mouth.

"Julian wanted her for himself. If Hawkins got the mail-order bitch, the boss thought he owed it to himself to get a little, too."

"He coulda shared."

"Not me. She looks like the type to give us all the clap."

Slocum considered getting off four killing shots before the outlaws responded. Any chance at that died when another joined the group. Slocum swung his six-shooter to cover Julian, only to have the other four crowd close around him and ruin a decent shot. He sank back down on the stone steps, trapped. Getting into the crypt, even if he shot off the lock, only trapped him. Pushing through the sheltering weeds made him an easy target. Wiping his nose as the pollen around him billowed into the air, he watched and waited. His chance would come soon.

"She isn't going to run toward town," Julian said. "More likely, she'll go deeper into the woods. That way." He pointed away from the crypt where Slocum hid.

"It wasn't our fault she got free, boss. Honest," said the man with the gold tooth. "She wiggled through a hole smaller than my damned fist."

"Right through the rock wall," piped up another. "It's like she turned to smoke."

"I'll smoke the lot of you if you don't find her soon. Sikes, Garcia, come with me. The rest of you go on back to camp.

She won't go that way, but as crazy as she is, who knows what she'll actually do."

Two men hurried off, glad to be away from their boss. Sikes—the man with the gold tooth—and his partner fanned out on either side of their leader and strode away, alert for anything moving through the grove. Slocum watched them disappear, then edged from his hiding place.

Polly's only chance to escape lay in getting out of the woods and away from Julian's gang. Slocum thought Julian was right about the woman hightailing it deeper into the forest rather than appealing to someone in town for help. She had no faith in a town where the marshal and bank president were brothers to the man who had brought such horror to her family. The rest of the citizens were under Hawkins's thumb and too frightened or bought off to help. And would anyone help the daughter of the man responsible for massacring half the town?

Even if she found someone in Espero to lend a hand, what could they do?

She had to reach the sheriff in another town or even a Texas Ranger. But Slocum knew telling the law what had happened to her and her family wouldn't be good enough. Even if a company of Rangers arrived and strung up everyone who had blighted her life, Polly wouldn't be happy. She wanted Hawkins for herself.

Just as Slocum wanted him.

He cut off to the right from the direction Julian and his men had taken. If he could find where Polly had been held prisoner, he might track her. Slocum had no reason to believe Julian wasn't a decent tracker or had one riding with him. That meant finding Polly amounted to Lady Luck smiling on him.

Slocum made his way into the woods long enough for the sun to sink low and bathe the world in twilight. The smaller forest critters popped out of their burrows and began foraging and feasting. More than one fox eyed him hungrily.

Distant crashing through the brush warned him of a rampaging javelina. And sitting and watching brought him the piece of luck he had been missing.

A small dark form moved along the path where he sat, simply waiting. If Slocum had been the hunted, he would have done the same thing, his pursuers moving faster along the cleared trail. They would overtake him and his freedom—and life—would be in peril.

The shadow moved parallel to the dirt track, then came out to look around.

"Hello, Polly," he said.

She jumped a foot. So startled, she took a step back, got her feet tangled, and fell heavily. She clutched a sharp-edged rock in one hand and clawed at the air like a mad cougar with the other.

"Settle down," he said. "Julian and his men went off in a different direction, but they might have circled around."

"John, how'd you find me?"

He held out his hand. She relaxed her claw and pulled herself up with his help. She stared at him for a moment, then collapsed against him, sobbing.

"They killed him for sure this time. They made me look while they nailed him up and—"

Her sobbing became uncontrollable.

"I saw. That's how I knew you were still alive. I found a footprint in the blood."

"I hate them, I hate them all!"

He wanted to ask if Julian had done anything to her other than forcing her to watch her pa's humiliation and death, but he held back. If she wanted to tell him, she would. Getting out of sight immediately trumped finding what had happened to her.

"There's got to be a place we can go to ground."

"I found a place yonder, by the river. Tree roots grew out and made a little cave on the bank."

He turned her in that direction and went along, letting her

lead the way even as he supported her. By the time they reached the river, she had recovered some of her gumption.

"There's my hidey-hole."

Slocum said nothing. The roots formed a dubious cave. Anyone on the far side of the stream could see them, and once inside, there was no way to go except out into the water, which would hinder an escape.

"It's not all that good, is it, John? It's all I could find being chased by a pack of jackals."

"Let's take a rest," he said. Slocum looked around, hunting for any sign that they had been spotted. In the dimness of the early evening, they might be safe. For a while.

After Polly worked her way into the muddy cave, Slocum followed, turned, and sat on a patch of moss to keep from sliding back out on the slick mud.

"I never expected you to find me," she said. "Thank you."

Slocum wasn't going to tell her it had been sheer luck. He put his arm around her and held her close. Polly's head rested on his shoulder. They said nothing as darkness became almost complete outside. He thought she had drifted off to sleep, but she finally said, "I thought we were hidden. I knew of an old ranch a couple miles off the road to Dexter. The owner had been a friend of Pa's, but Hawkins forced him to sell. Mr. Hulbert and his family moved. I never heard where. They were the smart ones."

"Your pa did right not to give in to a man like Hawkins."

"It cost him his wife and son and me my brother and Mama. And"—her sobs shook her now—"my pa. All I've got left is a worthless ranch and a need for revenge. You won't kill him, John. Don't kill him. I've *got* to."

"Staying alive long enough to figure how is the most important thing," he said.

The darkness closed in around him, bringing back impressions of the coffin. Water dripped on his head. He was underground. He was buried again.

"J-John, you tensed up. Did you hear something?"

"No, nothing."

He tried to relax but couldn't. Being buried alive had ignited his imagination so any dark, tight place became that coffin. Polly had rescued him. He concentrated on her being near, but he couldn't save her if he was buried. Could she save him if they were in the same grave?

"John! You're hurting me."

"Sorry," he said, taking his arm from around her shoulder. He had gripped down so hard his arm had lost circulation. Needles danced along it while he shook it to get feeling back. "I've never faced anyone like Hawkins before."

"Maybe we can kill him together?" Polly rested her head on his shoulder again and took his hand in hers. "How would we do that? Together?"

"How did you get away from Julian after they did that to your pa? He had a half-dozen men hunting for you."

"They took me to a stone hut. I don't know where it is. I just ran from it when I got free. The door was sturdy and locked on the outside, but I found a loose rock near the foundation. I knew what Julian intended to do to me, so I began digging as hard and fast as I could when I found it.

"The mortar came loose so I could pull out a stone about the size of my fist. I used that to chip away more mortar until the hole was big enough for me to stick my head out."

"Why didn't a guard see you? Or had Julian underestimated you and not left any?"

"Oh, there were guards. Three of them. But they had a friend to keep them company. A bottle of whiskey. For once I was glad the price in town is so low. The three of them couldn't have cobbled together enough change to trade for a silver dollar.

"So I kept digging and they kept passing the bottle around. My hole was finally big enough to squeeze through if I twisted my shoulders this way and that." She demonstrated. "Then I waited until they were snockered enough to pass out."

"Then you ran."

"I ran in the direction away from the front of the stone hut. It took me too long, though, because I hadn't gone a dozen yards when the hue and cry went up. Julian had come to . . . to take his due."

Slocum moved the gang leader to a spot just under Leonard Hawkins on his "to be shot like a mad dog" list. He owed Julian, but the things he had intended doing to Polly sealed his fate.

"I tried to run in a straight line to put as much distance between me and them as I could, but I got turned around and started veering off to my right. I think that was where I went since I splashed through the river. That was all turned around from what I thought, but I found this place and holed up here. You know the rest."

"You left to get out of the woods?"

"I left to find Julian. I was going to claw out his eyes and bash in his head."

Her voice had risen to a shrill pitch, but the constant rush of water masked any nosie they might make. Slocum waited for her to calm down, then said, "I'm thirsty. Join me at the river?"

"It's a long way to go, John. Why, it's almost five feet."

They slid from the tree root cave. Polly flopped belly down and scooped water into her mouth, Slocum knelt and lifted a palm dripping with water to his lips. What warned him he never knew, but he felt a presence behind him. He whirled about and flung the few drops of water in his right hand into Sikes's face. The man bellowed in surprise, momentarily showing his gold tooth.

Slocum fell into the river but got out his six-shooter. Using the shiny tooth as a target, he fired. The back of Sikes's head exploded as Slocum's aim was perfect.

"Oh, no, they've found us!"

Slocum shifted his aim and got off another shot at Sikes's partner—Garcia, Julian had called him. This round went high but put a hole through the brim of the man's hat. The nearness of the shot caused Garcia to miss Slocum. This split second gave Slocum enough time to cock his Colt and fire a third time.

He caught Garcia in the chest but didn't drop him. Garcia starting firing wildly, bullets splashing into the water all around. He grunted once when Slocum got off another shot at the man. This one took the outlaw in the neck. His six-gun fell from his hand, and he grabbed his throat. Blood squirted from between his fingers. He took a step forward, slipped on the mud, and toppled into the river. Slocum followed his body into the darkness, but he knew the man was dead.

"We've got to get out of here," he said.

No answer.

"Polly? Julian's not far off. The three of them went looking for you together."

He pulled himself out of the river and went to the bank, where the woman lay unmoving. He rolled her over. One of Garcia's wild bullets had caught her in the head, just above the ear. Other than a tiny spot of blood, she didn't have any obvious wound. But that bullet hole had done for her. She had died instantly.

Slocum stood and hunted for Julian. He would pay his debt for all he had done to the Neville family. Then Slocum would collect the rest of the debt from Leonard Hawkins.

16

Slocum went a little loco. He stumbled through the dark woods shouting Julian's name. If the gang leader showed, he would have a half-dozen men with him, but Slocum never considered that. The fight at the river had pushed him beyond his limits. Seeing Polly dead after all she had been through caused him to forget about any rational plan to fight Julian. He went into full guerrilla mode, the way he had been when riding with Quantrill during the war.

They had festooned themselves with eight six-shooters, then ridden at top speed screaming as loudly as they could. Firing one six-gun until it emptied, they would switch to the next and the next. A couple dozen guerrillas had the firepower of an entire Yankee company. The first time Slocum had ridden into battle like that, he had tried to measure each shot, make every one dead on target. He had come to realize he was trailing the others in his unit with this tactic. They lost themselves in the mindless fury of battle.

When he had done the same, the killing didn't come easier but he pushed away all concerns of whom he shot and why. Somehow, riding with Quantrill and the rest of his four hundred guerrillas in that spirit made him invincible. More than once he had charged into battle and been wounded, several times in one battle, and had never noticed until afterward. He had passed being an ordinary mortal and had become something more. He had become a killing machine with no feelings and no fear.

That fighting was years ago and amid a band of hardened killers, each outdoing the next when it came to bloodthirstiness. Slocum had repudiated such murder and those who had been his comrades in arms turned against him. That had been the last time Slocum had been a part of something greater— and the last time he had not been completely alone in the world. He depended on no one but himself now, and there hadn't been any call to murder entire towns filled with enemies.

Now he wished he had Quantrill and even Bloody Bill Anderson at his side. A quick foray, guns blazing, and Hawkins and Julian and the rest would be left in bloody tatters on the ground. But Quantrill had been ambushed in Kentucky and had died of his wounds in a Federal prison. Unlike the Ohio guerrilla, Slocum had learned from getting shot in the gut by his own side and lived to ride west.

Slocum slowed his furious assault through the woods and finally came to a halt. He caught his breath, then listened hard for sounds of others prowling about in the woods. To his left came small sounds, then a flurry of activity as small animals ran for cover. Someone had spooked them. With deliberate steps, he moved through the trees and saw the two men responsible for rousting the animals. They stood close together, talking in a low voice.

Slocum steadied his hand against the trunk of a maple tree and squeezed off a shot. The first man simply collapsed. For an instant his partner couldn't figure out what had happened. Then the same deadly accuracy was turned against him. Slocum dropped the second man, but not with a clean shot.

Moaning, kicking feebly, the outlaw tried to get to cover. With long, deliberate steps Slocum went to him.

"You're one of Julian's men," he said.

"Yeah, 'course. Somebody bushwhacked me. Get down or they'll get you like they got me and Larson."

"I should tell Julian what happened," Slocum said. "Where is he?"

"Back at the gravedigger's place." The man sat up and clutched his leg. "I'm bleedin' somethin' fierce. Give me a hand."

"Why?"

"Julian's payin' you, too, right?"

Slocum fired from the hip, but his aim was deadly. The bullet dug through the man's head and knocked him back onto the forest floor, as dead as his partner.

"Wrong," was all he said as he stripped the men of their six-shooters and jammed them into his belt.

He had become numb to killing after a while riding with Quantrill, but the feelings came back the longer he was away from the war. Now the moral outrage drained from him once more. When men like these needed killing, he discovered that a buried part of him was up to the task.

A trail through the woods led toward a stone hut. He started to let it be, then went around to the side and saw where Polly had pried stones loose from the mortar and squeezed through. The guard had been right. Anyone, even a small woman, snaking through a hole that size was a wonderment.

Memories of Polly again burning in his head, he took the trail and exited the woods, coming out at a different spot from where Hawkins and Miranda had entered the night before on the way to their wedding bed. Julian's camp was ahead. Two small cooking fires burned. He reloaded his Colt and returned it to his holster, then took the two six-guns from his belt. With one in each hand, he walked steadily into the camp. A man looked up.

Slocum fired twice with the pistol in his left hand. Another poked his head from under a blanket. A slug from each left and right pistols dispatched him. By now the others in the camp were coming awake, aware they were under attack. Slocum kept walking and firing, then tossed the emptied six-guns aside. He picked up two others dropped by men he had shot.

He turned, reversed his path through the camp, and took out three more. His steady pace and utter determination kept Julian's henchmen from shooting him before he killed them. It had been the same during the war riding with the guerrillas. The overwhelming firepower turned the tide. One last click on an empty chamber let him toss that captured weapon away.

A man who had been shot through the legs tried to crawl away. Slocum drew his Colt and walked to him. He shoved his foot down hard in the middle of the man's back. The scream cut through the still night.

"My legs. You're killin' me."

"Not yet," Slocum said. "Julian wasn't in camp."

"He's gone. Him and a couple others done left. They was ridin' out to a ranch for Hawkins."

"Which ranch?"

"I don't know." He screamed louder when Slocum put more weight on his back. The man's legs kicked more powerfully now as pain filled his body and brain. "The Box N. I don't know where that is. That's what they called it."

"Why was Julian sent there?"

"Hawkins wanted anything burned that showed somebody else owned the place. He was jumpin' the claim. Please, mister. I can't take this!"

Slocum let up on the pressure and stepped away. The cold killing spell had passed.

"If I see you here again, you're a dead man."

"I can't ride like this! My legs are all shot up."

Slocum cocked his Colt.

"Ride or die."

"Please, mister, I'll clear outta Espero. I promise you'll never see me again. Don't shoot me!"

Slocum bent and grabbed the man's collar to drag him along to the outlaws' remuda. From the way the man's legs flopped around, he wasn't playing possum. Slocum heaved and dumped him belly down over the back of a stallion, then unhitched the horse and gave it a swat on the rump. The man cried out but somehow held on as the horse raced away into the night.

A quick final circuit of the outlaw camp showed no one left alive. Slocum looked over at the funeral parlor. The building was dark, but Hawkins might be somewhere inside. Reloading as he walked, Slocum reached the side door through which so many coffins had been moved only that morning. Liam Neville had the right idea, but his execution had proven faulty, killing too many townspeople. Polly might never have lived down the shame of that mass killing, but she should never have been forced to find where Leonard Hawkins had buried her parents alive.

Slocum kicked in the door and looked around. Then he went inside. The building was as quiet as a grave—a grave with a corpse in it. Moving fast, he went room to room hunting for the undertaker. Hawkins was nowhere to be seen. That didn't surprise Slocum but it did disappoint him. He wanted this ended now.

Going out once more, the only place he could think to find Hawkins was in his bedroom crypt. But again Slocum failed to find the man.

The first hint of dawn showed on the horizon by the time Slocum returned to the outlaw camp. All he had to go on was the now-departed outlaw's claim that Julian had gone out to the Neville ranch. Slocum let the horses run free, then found his own and stepped up. The ride to the Box N was spent thinking over how he would approach Julian, how he would take his justice on the man for all his crimes.

Burying Slocum alive had become only one of many crimes for which he had to pay.

A mile from the ranch house, Slocum scented acrid smoke before he spotted the thin curl rising ahead. Hawkins had sent Julian here to remove any trace of legal occupation. The undertaker had gone from extortion to gain property to outright theft. And why not? The marshal was dead, even if Hawkins's youngest brother ever had had the gumption to enforce the law. Now Hawkins had simplified things and outright stole what he wanted.

Slocum drew his rifle from the saddle sheath and made certain the magazine carried its full fourteen rounds of .44-40 cartridges. He wished he had brought some of the six-shooters from the dead outlaws. Quantrill's method of overwhelming firepower would stand him in good stead now. With his Colt settled in his holster, he laid the rifle across his saddle and started toward the smoke.

As he rode closer, he saw only the smoldering ruins of the Neville house but no one responsible for setting the fire. The barn had long since been reduced to embers. He stared at the ruins, then came alert at the sound of a gunshot followed by loud whoops of glee. Slocum urged his horse forward, past the destroyed house and barn, to a grassy meadow badly in need of cattle to keep it cropped.

At the far side of the pasture Slocum saw three men on the ground. Their horses stood, nervously pawing the ground. As he rode closer, Slocum saw that the men had killed a cow and were butchering it for prime steaks. He lifted his rifle and fired, not at the men but at the three horses. His slug whistled between two of them but all he wanted was to create a stir, not kill a horse.

The shot caused one to rear and lash out with its front hooves at another. This caused the horses to bolt and run, leaving the three outlaws on foot.

Slocum rode closer. This time his rifle came to his shoulder for an accurate shot. He squeezed off a round and brought down a man standing with a bloody knife in his hand from the butchering. The other two slapped leather and threw lead in his direction. Slocum kept riding at a steady pace, then let out a cry and brought his horse to a gallop. His accuracy went away, but levering one round after another through the Winchester let him wing another of the men. He sagged to the ground, gripping his leg.

The injured outlaw fired two more rounds and came up empty. Then he came up dead. Slocum rushed within twenty yards and had an easy shot to the man's chest. The outlaw threw up his hands and fell over the bloody beef carcass.

Slocum turned his attention to the remaining outlaw. His anger boiled up. None of the three was Julian. Slocum rode past, wheeled about, and came back as the outlaw reloaded his six-gun. Three quick shots brought a yelp of pain to the outlaw's lips. He looked up and saw nothing but the bore of Slocum's rifle.

"You got me, mister. I surrender." The man dropped his pistol, and threw up his hands. He tried to stand but couldn't from the wound in his hip. "I'm hit. You don't need to finish me off. Just take me in so I can stand trial."

Slocum rode closer, keeping the front bead centered on the outlaw's chest. He didn't know if this man had helped trying to bury him alive. He didn't know what other crimes he had committed. If he rode with Julian and did Hawkins's bidding, his hands were red with more than a rustled cow's blood.

The man saw the expression on Slocum's face and tried to back away. His wound sent him crashing to the ground.

"You can't kill me out of hand. Don't do it. That'd make you a murderer!"

"Where's Julian?"

The man's sudden sly look made Slocum pull the trigger. The bullet took the man's life even as Slocum bent low and hung on to his horse's neck. The movement saved his life. He urged the pinto to a gallop away from the edge of the woods, where an ambusher had tried to back-shoot him.

From the way the dead outlaw had reacted, the would-be killer was the man Slocum sought.

Slocum rode as far as he thought safe from a shot coming from the woods. He brought his rifle up and studied the lay of the land, deciding where Julian would have been. A notch in the woods showed a trail followed by cattle to get to another pasture. That was where the outlaw leader would be since he had no call to rummage about in the undergrowth before Slocum showed up, guns blazing.

"Julian!" Slocum waited to see if there was any response. "You buried me alive. You're going to pay for that."

"You could have saved everyone trouble by staying buried," the outlaw shouted back.

Slocum adjusted his aim a few inches and caught sight of a red bandanna amid the green bushes. He squeezed the trigger. The familiar kick satisfied him. The shot felt good. But he had to be sure.

"I'm coming for you, Julian. You can run, but I'll track you to the ends of the earth."

Getting no response, Slocum began riding back toward the spot where the three outlaws had butchered the Box N cow. He relied on his sense of a good shot. It had *felt* right. But that didn't mean he had killed Julian. At this range, such a shot would have been half skill and half miracle.

The notch in the trees proved to be a large trail, as Slocum had thought. He turned his attention to the left side of the trail, hunting for any ambush Julian might deliver. A wounded rat fought hardest.

Only Slocum's sense was wrong. Julian stepped out from the right side of the trail, unharmed by the exchange of fire. He sighted in and fired at Slocum just as the horse reared. Slocum kicked free of the stirrups and let the horse throw him. Prepared for the impact, Slocum landed hard on his back, then jerked about and rolled away. Bullets whined off rocks and dug up tiny divots as he kept moving to take shelter in the woods.

Slocum settled down behind a tree with a trunk big enough to shelter a couple men. He chanced a look around one side, then rolled and brought his rifle to bear shooting around the other. The rifle bucked and Julian cursed, but it wasn't a hit. Slocum knew he had been wrong before, but this time he wasn't. He had come close but had missed.

Working his way to standing and bracing the rifle against the tree, he began to fire in brackets. To the left of where he thought Julian stood, to the right, and then between the two. After each trio of shots, he moved his targeting to flush out the outlaw.

He lowered his rifle when the magazine came up empty. Slocum cursed under his breath since he had no idea what had become of Julian. The outlaw might have disappeared into thin air, carried away on the muggy breeze blowing across the pasture. Resting his rifle against the tree, Slocum drew his six-shooter, then considered how best to go after Julian. He picked up the rifle in his left hand and used it to poke through the brush as he made his way closer to the trail between pastures.

"You turn tail and run like a dog, Julian?" He rustled the bushes off to his left with the rifle. His ruse worked.

The hatched-faced outlaw had to step from behind a tree on the far side of the trail to get a shot at where he thought Slocum moved.

Slocum lifted his Colt, dropped the rifle, and fanned off all six shots. Not all hit Julian. Enough did to make the outlaw groan and fall back. Slocum reloaded, picked up his rifle, and wished he had the ammo for it, too. It still proved useful pushing aside the thick brush so he could concentrate on the outlaw.

Julian burst out of the brush. To Slocum's surprise, the man was mounted. The outlaw rode bent low, firing as he went. Slocum fired at the outlaw as he raced back toward the smoking ruins of the Neville house. When he came up empty, he fished around for more ammo. He was out. He had more in his saddlebags, but Julian would be long gone by the time he found his horse and reloaded.

With his fingers between his lips, he let out a long, loud whistle. His horse came trotting up, looking at him fearfully. Slocum took his time gentling the pinto. Then he took out the boxes of ammo and reloaded both his rifle and the six-shooter. He swung into the saddle and went after Julian. Wounded, the man wasn't likely to hightail it anywhere but Espero.

Slocum considered that luck had finally come his way. He had escaped without any new holes in his hide and knew where Julian rode. If luck really smiled on him, both Julian and Hawkins would be together, and he could dispatch both at the same time.

"This time," Slocum said softly, "you're going to need two graves." He headed back to Espero and the inevitable showdown.

17

Slocum rode straight for Hawkins's funeral parlor. He smiled grimly as he rode closer. He had guessed Julian's destination. The man's lathered horse stood out back, near the camp where Slocum had gone through killing his henchmen like he was a farmer with a scythe cutting wheat. Julian had to be panicked now. That made him more dangerous. It also meant he wouldn't be thinking straight.

"Lead me to Hawkins, you son of a bitch," Slocum said softly as he dismounted.

He hefted his rifle and went into the mortuary. He heels clicked on the floor as he moved with increasing determination. When he came to the viewing room, he found pieces of a dozen coffins scattered about. These were the remnants of the three dozen coffins Hawkins had hammered together for the townspeople Neville had killed. He had enough planks left over for half a dozen more. Slocum kicked through the pile but found nothing to tell him where Julian and Hawkins were.

In the dining room, he paused. Food remained on the table from the meal he had watched served on Miranda's wedding night. The number of dead rats on the table in front of Hawkins's plate showed only his food had been poisoned. Miranda's plate had been licked clean.

He swung around, his rifle rising to cover whoever sneaked up on him from behind.

"John, don't! Please, don't!" Miranda looked gaunt, and her hands shook as she held them in front of her, palms outward, as if to push him away.

"Where is he?"

"I don't know. I really don't."

"I want Julian, too. He rode in all shot up. Where is he?"

"I didn't hear him ride up. He . . . he's with Leonard, if he's anywhere."

"And you don't know where Hawkins is."

Slocum sighted directly between her heaving bosoms. He had no intention of shooting her. If this loosened her tongue so he found out what he wanted, however, the fright was worth it.

"I don't. He is so strange. So very strange." She pressed her hand to her breasts. "He gave me this." A tug brought up a large brass key hung from a delicate gold chain.

"What does it open?"

"He didn't tell me, but he laughed. It was terrible, that laugh was terrible! You don't know what a monster he is, John. You can't."

Slocum knew. He went to the woman, wary of her being used as bait in a trap. No sign of Hawkins or Julian in the room behind her emboldened him. With a quick grab, he caught the key and pulled it from around her neck. She let out a tiny gasp as the metal links cut into the back of her neck.

"It opens a padlock," he said. "A big one. What's locked up around here? And why would he want you to have the key?"

"I don't know. He's so generous and so frightening at the same time. He's given me boxes of jewelry."

"And a handmade coffin for a wedding gift," Slocum finished for her.

"That, too." She closed her eyes and wove about unsteadily. Slocum made no move to support her. Miranda reached out and used the wall to keep from collapsing. "He's taken it all from the people he's buried. Even this."

She held up her wedding ring. The sparkle off the huge stone blinded Slocum for a moment. He blinked, wary of a trap. Miranda simply stared at it as if it were a crystal ball and she read her fortune in it—and that fortune was bleak.

"He made me ring the bell, but on the morning of the funerals, he had me stop and come rob the bodies. There were so many he couldn't do it by himself. I took necklaces and watches and rings."

Miranda dropped to her knees, put her face in her hands, and sobbed openly.

"What more is there?"

She looked up with teary eyes and shook her head. "What do you mean, John? That's monstrous, robbing dead people!"

"But nothing you haven't done," he said harshly. "You would have enjoyed running your fingers over the gold and silver. What has really upset you about him?"

"Nothing went right. Nothing after I found he wasn't in Dexter Junction. At least, he didn't lie about being rich."

"That was why you wanted to marry him. And why your partner was going to kill him. You'd inherit it all as his wife."

"Harry put more than enough strychnine on his food to kill him that night, but he must have known. He never touched a bite."

Slocum had seen the pantomime Hawkins had put on for her benefit. He didn't tell her he had seen her partner or any part of the meal. It was better to see what she willingly told him.

"If he'd eaten it, he would have died and there wouldn't have been a repeat of our awful wedding night. We made love, if you can call it that, in a large casket. In a burial vault! The walls were painted with grotesque figures doing the vilest things. And he wanted to do each and every one of them with me! Why couldn't he have eaten the poison?"

Slocum had little sympathy for her. She wiped at her tears and tried to stand. Her legs almost gave way, then she made it to a chair and sat heavily. As Miranda composed herself, Slocum looked at the key. Hawkins wasn't giving her the key to any treasure. He wasn't that kind of man. This would open a world of pain for her, but what lock did it fit?

"He's treated me like a slave since our wedding night. A sex slave! He has the most depraved appetites."

"You would have killed him for his money. How many times have you and your partner Harry done this?"

Miranda sat up straighter and stared right at him, head high, as she said, "Leonard would have been the fourth. He was also the wealthiest. Most of the men lied about their money."

"Fancy that," he said, not trying to keep the sarcasm from his voice.

Slocum walked around the room, looking at cabinets. What locks were on them were small, so small the key wouldn't even fit. He left the room and wandered through the funeral home, looking at every cabinet and drawer that had been locked. This key fit none of them. He returned to where Miranda still sat. Her hands were clasped in her lap and she looked like a contrite schoolgirl now caught cheating.

In that instant, he almost felt sorry for her. Almost.

She was a thief and a murderer, even if her partner had done the actual killing. If Hawkins had been on the up-and-up, she and Harry would have killed him with poison, then moved on when the estate had been settled.

Slocum bounced the key up and down in his palm.

"Hawkins knew you tried to kill him, didn't he?"

"He never said anything, but he must have. He made

some comment about strangers in town and how Espero had a way of making them disappear."

"When was the last time you talked to your partner?"

"Last night. Harry wanted to try again, but things became so chaotic after that rancher blew up half the townspeople, he didn't get a good chance."

"Hawkins knew from the start," Slocum said. "The food on the table shows that."

"The rats ate it and died. I . . . I haven't been able to clean them up. I just couldn't bear it."

"Is he your husband?"

"I don't know. He said the man with the Bible was a parson."

"Not Hawkins, Harry. Were you married to him?"

"Of course not," she said indignantly. "That wouldn't have been right, me being married and then getting married to all those men."

Slocum tried to make sense out of that twisted sense of propriety and couldn't. Miranda wouldn't commit adultery, but murder and robbery were all right. He bounced the key again, then said, "I know what this opens. There's a crypt with weird figures carved on it out in the woods."

"The marriage crypt," she said, shuddering at the memory.

"That's plain on the outside. I found another one that's hidden away and has a hefty lock on the door. I was going to break in, but Julian's men came along and I had to high-tail it." He made no effort to explain what had happened to Liam Neville—or Polly.

"Leonard hinted there were many scattered throughout the woods. I have no idea what he used them for. He assured me the . . . the marriage crypt was unsullied before our night there."

Slocum knew of one other, where Neville had been cru-cified. Hawkins had unlimited money and time to build his sepulchers. Only a thorough search of the forest would reveal them all. Slocum heaved a sigh. Not only wasn't that worth it, but he wanted nothing more than to send the locations of all those crypts to the grave with Hawkins.

He took her hand and led the woman from the funeral parlor. She shied away from the carnage in Julian's camp. Slocum ignored the stench and flies as he single-mindedly plowed on to find the buried crypt with the padlocked door. Miranda let out a tiny gasp as they passed the first crypt. Slocum got his bearings and cut through the woods, finding an occasional game trail that made the going easier. He had a good sense of direction but wished he had a compass. The dense foliage often cut off his view of the sun and made staying on a direct course difficult. But when they reached the grassy spot where he had seen Julian and the others in his gang as they prepared to hunt down Polly, he homed in on the marble steps.

"It's overgrown with weeds," Miranda said. "Are you sure this is where—oh."

Miranda put her hand to her mouth when she saw that Slocum had slipped the key into the padlock and turned. It clicked open and hung by the hasp. He pulled off the lock and tossed it aside. The door opened on well-oiled hinges. The curious odor inside made his nose wrinkle, but it wasn't unpleasant.

"What's in there?"

"Something Hawkins gave you the key for," Slocum said.

He fished around for his tin of lucifers and took one out. He had only a few left. Holding the match high as it flared, he saw the layout was similar to the other crypts. On a low table beside the door stood a kerosene lamp. He worked to get the wick lighted, then held the lamp high to see the entire room.

"Those odd figures," Miranda said. "Those are hieroglyphics. Leonard told me the ancient Egyptians used them as a kind of writing."

"If this is a treasure map and he wanted you to decipher it, you'd better get started." Slocum couldn't make head nor tail of the strange figures but at least they weren't doing unspeakable things to each other. He turned his attention to a stone bier in the middle of the large room. "This looks like a mummy."

"He told me about those, too. The Egyptians preserved their dead in some peculiar fashion so they would last forever." Miranda moved closer, then gasped, "Harry!"

Slocum lowered the lamp and pulled back gauzy bandages on the mummy's face. He had never gotten a good look at Miranda's partner, but he wasn't going to argue with her. The man hadn't been dead too long but had a gaunt, drawn look.

"The containers beside the bier are canopic jars containing the brains and other internal organs."

Slocum whirled, only to find himself at a disadvantage because he held the lamp in his gun hand.

"You'll be dead before you can drop the lamp," Julian said. He held a shotgun. "If it was up to me, you'd be dead right now."

"You certainly inflicted great injury on my right-hand man," Leonard Hawkins said, taking great pleasure from springing his trap so successfully. He held a small-caliber pistol on Miranda. "My dear, your lover will be preserved for all eternity. Egyptian mummies are thousands of years old. When I seal this door, he will be consigned to the far future."

"Don't, Slocum. I don't care what he says. I'll shoot you down if you go for that hogleg." Julian leaned back to brace the butt of the shotgun stock against the door frame. The wounds in his left arm had to be painful. Slocum saw a couple oozed blood, but this wouldn't prevent Julian from discharging the shotgun if the need arose.

"Do you intend to kill me and suck my brains out through my ear, too?" Slocum asked.

"You do not understand the improvements I've made to the ancients' techniques. No, Slocum, I remove the brains through the nose. And I do so before the interred is dead."

"You drilled into Harry's brain while he was still alive?" Miranda collapsed to the floor.

"You show some intellect now, my dear. I wish it had been more apparent earlier. You might not have tried your ridiculous scheme with your lover. Poisoning a man who works with deadly chemicals and has learned to sniff out the cause of death for even the most innocent looking of corpses? While I would have missed two glorious nights of sexual rhapsody with you, both you and he would be alive yet if you had not tried to kill me using your mail-order bride plot." Hawkins stepped away. "And you also, Mr. Slocum."

Slocum tensed, ready to throw the lamp at Julian and take his chances with the small pistol Hawkins clutched in his meaty grip.

"You have been quite a thorn in my side. And if you try throwing, or even dropping, that lamp, I will shoot lovely Miranda. Would you be responsible for her death?"

"She doesn't mean anything to me."

"Not like the poor, departed Polly Neville. Yes, Julian had reported her death. You two were quite close, I suspect. But don't move a muscle, Slocum. Julian is weakening from the wounds you inflicted on him and will likely draw back on the trigger if he begins to pass out. You might be fast with that gunfighter's weapon of yours, but no one is faster than buckshot."

"What are you going to do, Hawkins? Bury me alive again? That didn't work out so good for you the first time."

"When at first you don't succeed, try, try again." Hawkins fired at him.

Slocum flung the lamp, twisted to the side, and wrapped his arms around Miranda, knocking her out of the way of Julian's shotgun blast. He felt a hot crease across his back as one shot hit. Then he had an armful of struggling woman—in the complete darkness.

"Damn, he's locked us in." Slocum scrambled to his feet,

got tangled in Miranda's skirts, and almost fell. He braced himself against the bier and its contents.

He yanked back as if he had been burned by contact with Harry's mummy. Slocum got turned around as he stepped away and found himself uncertain which way the door lay. He drew his pistol, but he had no idea where he aimed. A shot inside a stone crypt might be deadly. The slug's ricochet might hit him or Miranda.

"Find the lamp. We can light it."

"It's smashed, John. When you dropped it, the glass broke and all the kerosene spilled onto the floor." She let out a very unladylike curse. "I cut myself on a piece of the glass chimney."

Slocum fought down panic. He had been buried in a coffin. This was a roomier crypt. But the darkness! He felt as if a giant's fist punched his chest with every breath he took. That was ridiculous. Running out of air so quickly wasn't possible. His terror subsided as he fought it back like some towering, all-devouring beast.

"What are we going to do? I don't want to die!"

"Be quiet. Save our air," Slocum said. "I'm not sure this tomb is sealed tight enough for us to worry about that, but until I find out, keep quiet."

Her soft sobs told Slocum where she was. He ran his hand along the bier. The door was at one end or the other. Slipping his pistol back into its holster, he held out his hands and explored their stony prison.

"Got it. The door's in front of me."

He ran his hands over the splintery wood. The door held against his hardest kicks. He tried his shoulder against it and all he got was a bruised shoulder. Relying on brute strength wouldn't get them out. He worked his fingers around the edge, hunting for hinges to attack. Then he remembered the door swung outward, so the hinges were outside and away from his tinkering.

"Can't you shoot the lock?"

"The wood's an inch thick and hard. Remember the lock? It was a padlock. I'd have to shoot through the wood and the lock. Unless I had a mountain howitzer, no amount of shooting is going to affect that lock."

He sank down. Mind tumbling with ideas to escape, he finally admitted none of them were plausible. Being in the dark was the worst of it. Somehow, this turned the air stuffy and his lungs strained more as if they sucked in liquid fire. Slocum took out a lucifer and struck it. He had closed his eyes against the flare so he wasn't blinded like Miranda.

She held up an arm to protect her eyes as she knelt at the side of the bier. He saw where the kerosene lamp had smashed on the floor. Miranda had been right about the volatile liquid seeping away into the floor. Only a small discoloration remained to show where it had stained the rock floor before being thirstily absorbed beneath.

Slocum scowled as the match burned his fingers. He tossed the tiny stub away. He had seen what he feared most. There wasn't any way from the crypt other than the door leading in. For the life of him, he couldn't imagine that Hawkins would have put in a back door or some escape tunnel. The ancient Egyptians might have hidden a chamber for a king to keep the robbers from looting the crypt, but that chamber still had only one exit.

Slocum leaned back against the solid wood door that gave them their only way out.

"We can dig out, John. I saw how the kerosene went between the floor stones. We can tunnel out!"

He heard Miranda scrabbling about, trying to get purchase on a stone. When she did, a gasp of despair filled the chamber.

"The ground's too hard to dig through," he said.

"It's harder than the stone. Maybe if I used the edge of the stone as a spade, I can get out that way."

Sounds of frantic burrowing slowly subsided until all he

heard were Miranda's gasping and the pounding of his own heart in his ears.

"We're going to die in here, aren't we, John?"

He made his way to her in the dark, fumbling a bit as he found the stone she had removed. A quick brush of his hand over the dirt showed only shallow grooves. Digging out would take forever.

"Hold me, John. I can't stand it much longer unless you hold me."

He worked around, leaned against the bier, and took the woman in his arms. Her warmth and soft breath gusting across his neck as she lay her head on his shoulder calmed him. No decent escape plan came to him, but he held his panic in check.

"I never thought I'd die like this," she said.

"We're still alive. I want to get Hawkins in my sights and pull the trigger."

"He left you with your six-shooter. Why?"

Slocum kept silent on that. He had been buried with his six-gun before. Hawkins and probably Julian took special pleasure in the idea that their victims might choose to kill themselves rather than die in the dark of suffocation. He had his gun and enough ammo to erase the misery both he and Miranda would be feeling when the air finally became too stale.

"I got out of being buried alive by them before."

"Can you do it again?"

Slocum bit his tongue, wishing he had never mentioned that. Polly and her brother had saved him. Both of them were dead now. The whole damned Neville family was dead, shot down, crucified, or . . . buried alive.

"We'll need to think of some other way." He felt her stirring against him. "This time there's more air, and we've got plenty of room."

"But we're going to die. I know it. I want my last minutes to be something more than stark fear."

Her hand moved down to his leg, then worked up to his crotch. She began rhythmically squeezing, pumping him up, getting him rock hard. Straining against the fabric of his jeans, he felt confined in all ways now. And then he was suddenly free. Miranda had popped the fly buttons and let him come leaping out, like a racehorse at the starting line.

"You understand what I mean," she said in a husky voice. "If we have to use up the air, let's do it fast. And hard. Very hard to make us both forget."

She clamped down around his erection and began moving her hand up and down slowly. For his part, Slocum reached around and undid one button after another on her blouse. Then he burrowed about and found one warm mound of woman flesh beneath the loosened fabric. As she held on to him, he squeezed down on her. The tiny nip at the crest of the fleshy mountain hardened as he toyed with it, twisting and tweaking until he felt the distant throb of her pulse in that rubbery flesh.

Moving in the dark proved easy enough since they both clung to each other in intimate ways. Slocum shucked off his gun belt and opened the button at his waist so he could scoot down his pants. Lifting his ass off the floor to skin out of the jeans proved too awkward.

He used his grip on her boob to lift her.

"Stand up," he ordered.

Together they got to their feet. Slocum bent over and licked and suckled at the woman's chest, leaving a wet trail that went from the deep valley between her breasts, down to the well of her navel, and then lower until he was thwarted by her skirts. He came at her from the other direction now. His hand found the trembling pillar of a leg, and he worked upward under her skirt. The flesh of her thighs was already damp from juices leaking from her interior.

When he thrust two fingers into her, she cried out. Miranda began grinding her crotch down into his hand, seeking to drive him even deeper. His fingers wiggled about with her center. Warm juices lubricated his fingers and let him stroke over the scalloped flaps of her nether lips. Catching one between his thumb and forefinger, he ran slowly from top to bottom and back.

He had to support her as she sagged in reaction.

"I almost came, John. Almost. Don't you dare stop now."

"Is this all you want?" He twirled his fingers around within her. "Or do you want more?"

"This, this!" She tugged on his steely length, pulling it toward her. "I want this in me, making me forget everything but—"

She cried out when he shoved his thumb into her and used his middle finger on a different entrance to her body. He kept up the dual assault until he could turn her about so she leaned over the bier.

With a wide sweep of his arm, he shoved Harry's mummy from the bier. In the darkness, she couldn't see it, but he wanted nothing to distract her from what he did from behind. She lay forward across the stone slab, arms outstretched to tighten her belly and backside.

He explored a bit more, spreading her ass cheeks and probing with his fingers. She sobbed and rewarded him with a wider stance. When she reached back to hold herself open to him, Slocum worked the tip of his shaft against a tightly clenched hole. A gradual pressure moved him forward, a fraction of an inch, a half inch, deeper. All the while Miranda cried out for more.

He finally penetrated her with the thick purpled head at the end of his manhood. Slocum had to pause. Heat boiled from her interior. Never had he felt such tightness around him. When she began pushing back so her curves fit into the hollow of his belly and upper legs, he pressed forward. Not hurrying, he sank inch by inch into her until both lost all hope for rational thought.

The fury boiling in his loins threatened to erupt. But he wasn't going to let it happen. He fought for control so he could relish the pleasures Miranda so wantonly offered up. Drawing back as slowly as he had entered, he finally had to pause again and regroup.

She cried out constantly now, cursing and sobbing, shouting and demanding he return to fill her to overflowing. This time his entry was faster. And the retreat? Twice as fast. His new thrust moved with more power and finally he was pistoning until he reached the point of no return. One hand gripped her waist and the other pressed into the stone bier. Eyes closed or open didn't matter. He felt the woman around him, the stone slab sliding as he thrust even more deeply into her from behind until he could take it no more. He exploded, slathering her innards with his seed.

Miranda crammed herself back onto his impaling shaft, reached down, and began fingering herself, then cried out in release. Slocum thought he was going to be crushed flat as her inner muscles tightened so much there was no room left for him. But having spent, he was already going limp. He let her soaring desires fade and pulled back until he flopped from her. He kept his hands on the rounded curves of her behind, stroking and feeling the warmth of her flesh until she simply sprawled forward, as exhausted as he was.

"I've never felt anything like that before," she said. "Too bad it'll be the last time."

Slocum put his hands on either side of her body and leaned forward. He shifted his weight and rubbed against her bare bottom.

"As good as you are, John, you're not going to get hard enough soon enough."

"I know how to get out," he said. He thought she climaxed again at those words.

18

"I know how we can get out," Slocum repeated.

"What? How? You figured it out but screwed me first?"

"During," Slocum said. "It came to me while we were doing it."

Miranda laughed, and it was almost cheerful. He heard a note of hysteria rising in her voice but she tried to keep it light. "I inspired you?"

"The stone slab on the bier moved."

"Lots of things moved, but I don't understand. That's where Harry was laid out, but you must have pushed him off."

"If we lift the stone slab, we can use it as a battering ram. I'll light a match, we can get ourselves set and then run at the door as hard as we can. It's going to be heavy, and we'll have to do this together. I don't think I could lift the slab alone."

"I hate Hawkins so for what he's done, I'll do anything."

"Close your eyes. Here comes the light."

He struck a match, let it flare, then opened his own eyes. The light hurt because he had been plunged into such intense blackness for so long. Slocum couldn't help looking at

Miranda. Her blouse was open and her breasts hung out.
Her skirt was bunched up around her waist, and he caught
sight of her sleekly rounded behind as she turned from him
toward the door. This reminded him of why he had struck
the lucifer. He took in everything he needed to know as the
light flickered and burned out.

"We're five feet from the door. I'll get on the far side of
the slab. It's already partially off the pedestal. We lift it and
then run for all we're worth."

He knew they might get only one shot at it if the stone
proved too heavy for Miranda. Her anger at Hawkins fueled
one attempt. Two might be out of the question, even if it
meant saving their lives. He edged around the bier and
worked his fingers under the slab and tried to lift. Too heavy
for him alone. Kicking away Harry's mummy, he braced his
feet on the floor.

"You saw where to pick up the slab. Ready?"

"I'm ready to kill Leonard!"

Slocum counted down, they lifted, and he yelled, "Run!
Run for all you're worth!"

His foot slipped when he broke the canopic jar with Harry's sucked-out brains in it. He strained every muscle in his
belly and back heaving himself forward. He hoped they were
on target because Miranda wasn't holding up her side of the
slab. It had to weigh a couple hundred pounds.

Time flowed strangely. Slocum imagined himself trapped
in this crypt to die, if not from suffocation, then from lack
of water and starvation. Seeing nothing. Every breath a
nightmare. Miranda would become increasingly fearful and
might go mad. *He* might go crazy as death neared.

All this flashed through his head, and then the shock of
their crude battering ram echoed all the way up his arms and
jolted him. The crunching sound of wood being splintered
was drowned out by his own cry of triumph as light and air
gushed through the destroyed door. They had knocked it off
its hinges so it hung half open, held only by the lock.

"We should have hit it nearer the lock," Slocum said.

Miranda rushed into his arms, crying and laughing. She clung fiercely to him and said, "You did it. You got us free." Pulling back a few inches, she looked up and said, "You have green eyes. This is the first time a man's made love to me when I didn't know the color of his eyes beforehand."

She kissed him hard. He enjoyed the moment of jubilation, then pushed her away.

"We need to get out of here," he said.

While he doubted Hawkins had posted a guard outside, he had no idea how many of Julian's gang remained. If they had the sense God gave a goose, they would have all hightailed it by now. The ones he hadn't killed he had wounded and sent on their way out of town. That should have been warning enough.

He and Miranda stumbled past the broken door and on hands and knees made their way to the forest floor. Slocum looked back at the crypt. The faint light filtering in showed the hieroglyphics and the foot of Harry's mummy. The sight hardened Slocum's resolve even more. Nothing Leonard Hawkins could do now would save him.

"He won't be at the funeral parlor," Miranda said. "He might be at the cemetery. He spends much of his free time there."

"He could be anywhere in this forest," Slocum said. The Hill Country was festooned with heavily wooded areas like this, able to hide any number of Hawkins's crypts. "I need to figure out where he and Julian would go."

"The cemetery," Miranda said without hesitation.

Slocum set off down the path, but he wanted to be certain Miranda wasn't trying to send him on a wild-goose chase. Her determination to kill Hawkins matched his own. She protested as he went back to the mortuary. Slocum checked his pistol, then went inside to search it.

When he came out, Miranda stood with her fists on her hips. She glared at him, then silently pointed down the road toward the graveyard.

"I'm not so sure," Slocum said. "Things have come unraveled. Hawkins isn't going to keep doing things as he always has."

"Why not? He thinks we're goners. He killed Harry. I heard tell that the marshal was dead. As much as the man made my spine crawl, he had guts enough to speak up to his brother. That worthless bank president will play fetch until the day one of them dies." Miranda took a deep breath, realized her blouse was unbuttoned, and then chastely fastened what buttons were left. "I want this to be Hawkins's last day on earth. I don't care what happens to his brother."

Slocum fetched his horse and swung up into the saddle. He drew his rifle and checked it.

"Where's my horse?" Miranda asked.

"Find one and come with me or stay here." Slocum turned his pony's face and trotted off, heading for the cemetery.

Miranda screamed at him, but he ignored her. She would only get in his way. He brought the horse to a gallop when he spotted the sign pointing to the boneyard. A few trees spotted the hills and most had new graves near them. Liam Neville's slaughter had added a significant number of new residents to this city of the dead.

Slocum pulled out his rifle when he saw a horse tethered to a tree limb. He hit the ground running and rushed up the slope, keenly aware of every sound, every movement, every smell around him. Death rose from the graves, mingled with freshly turned earth. He didn't see the horse's rider but did hear the sound of a shovel digging into the ground.

When he topped the rise, he saw the outlaw leader working to throw dirt into a grave. Beside Julian grew a stack of glittering gold and silver jewelry.

Slocum never gave Julian a chance to draw. He pulled the rifle stock into his shoulder and fired. But his usual patience and skill were pushed aside by his towering rage at the outlaw. He jerked the trigger, and the shot went high and to the left. Julian looked up, saw Slocum, and reacted instantly. He dropped the shovel and dived over the small mound of dirt beside the grave.

"I never took you for a back-shooter, Slocum," the outlaw called out. "Let's do this right. Face to face. Whoever's quickest on the draw wins."

"You're nothing but a graverobber," Slocum said, levering in another round and walking steadily toward Julian. Only when the outlaw poked his head over the top of the dirt mound and fired off a round in his direction did Slocum react.

He dived to the right, landed on his belly, and waited.

"I'll split it with you, Slocum. We don't have a quarrel, you and me."

"Why didn't Hawkins steal all that jewelry before burying the corpses?" Slocum only wanted to draw out the outlaw so he could get a decent shot. The reasons why Hawkins neglected his main source of income were of no concern.

"Hawkins gave me a map to the graves where he didn't rob the corpses first. He was so rushed getting so many buried, he wasn't alone with the bodies for long and that bitch of a wife wasn't too good stripping off the jewelry. And then some of them damned families crowded in to see the dead. They wouldn't take kindly to him removing their heirlooms. Things were kinda rushed, thanks to Neville."

"That's why he needed you, to do the jobs he didn't have time for." Slocum squeezed down on the trigger, just short of firing a round. One of those jobs was burying him alive.

"We don't have to end it like this, Slocum. You're one stone killer. I saw what you did to most of my gang, the ones that weren't chased off. Me and you, we can be partners. We're cut from the same cloth."

Slocum shifted his aim to the far end of the dirt mound as Julian popped up. This time he fired perfectly. Julian stood upright, dropped his six-shooter, gripped his chest, and stared at Slocum in surprise.

"We coulda been hell on wheels, Slocum, you and me." He fell forward, toppling into the open grave. The sound of him hitting the pinewood coffin lid echoed across the wind-swept cemetery. Then there was nothing.

Slocum got to his feet and advanced slowly. He peered down into the grave. Julian sprawled facedown on the coffin. A red stain spread on his back. Slocum's slug had gone clean through him. He took aim again to add one final round. Julian had died too fast and this shot was going to be nothing but pure cussedness on Slocum's part.

Then he froze.

"She dies if you don't throw down your rifle. Add your six-gun to the pile on the ground."

Slocum turned slowly. Leonard Hawkins had Miranda in a headlock using his left arm. In his right fist he held a small-caliber pistol. A thousand things ran through Slocum's head. Such a tiny gun was close to worthless against him, but should Hawkins place it to the woman's head, he could kill her in an instant.

"You can shoot her, but I'll gun you down."

"I was afraid you'd take that road," Hawkins said. He shoved the gun into Miranda's back and pushed her forward, using her body as a shield. "Are you willing to kill her to get to me?"

"Yes."

Slocum lifted the rifle, intending to blast through Miranda since there wasn't a good shot to Hawkins's head. What he didn't expect was Hawkins shoving her forward so that she stumbled. She threw out her arms for balance and one groping hand hit his rifle. The round discharged, the slug digging into the ground to one side of Hawkins.

"Got you, Slocum," Hawkins exulted. He raised his pistol to fire, but as Miranda had ruined Slocum's shot, she kicked out and struck Hawkins in the knee to knock him off balance.

The undertaker yelped and twisted to favor the injured leg. Slocum went for his six-shooter as Hawkins fired. Slocum winced as the slug ripped into his right arm. The wound didn't amount to a hill of beans, but he couldn't close his hand. He grabbed for his six-shooter with his left hand.

Miranda kept Hawkins from firing a second time, kicking backward like a mule. She caught him in the belly and sent him staggering. Slocum awkwardly got out his six-shooter but found himself dealing with the woman as she crawled forward to get away from her attacker. He tried to sidestep but fell into the grave, landing atop Julian. Hawkins got off another round. Miranda joined Slocum in the grave.

"Oh, no," she said. She turned pale at having piled on top of a dead man in a grave.

"Can you shoot?"

"What? I have fired a gun before."

Slocum swung his left hand around and handed her his Colt. He winced as he pressed into the wound. He pulled off his bandanna and tied it around his biceps. Blood still oozed out, but he wasn't going to bleed to death.

"What do you want me to do?"

"Pop up, if you see Hawkins, shoot at him. If you don't, wait until I get out of the grave. Then you run like hell back to your horse, climb up, and start riding."

"Where?"

"Anywhere that's not Espero," Slocum said.

Miranda poked her head up, rested the six-gun on the edge of the grave, but didn't shoot.

"I don't see him. He went back over the rise."

"Get ready," Slocum said. He reached down and found Julian's pistol, then nodded.

Miranda went over the lip of the grave and hurried off. Slocum covered her but saw no trace of Hawkins. He thought he understood the man well enough to know all the bravado would have drained from him. His henchman was dead, his hostage escaped, and all he had to defend himself was a small pistol.

Slocum gripped Julian's gun with both hands. Some

feeling came back into his gun hand but he wasn't sure he could trust it in a serious fight.

Slocum circled the hill and came up on the far side. He hoped Hawkins would go after the woman. Using Miranda as bait rankled, but not killing Hawkins would be worse than losing her. He had given her the chance to fight back. His Colt Navy would not fail her. Hefting Julian's pistol, he worried this ill-kept weapon would misfire or otherwise go bust.

Being this close to Hawkins, Slocum would use the gun to bludgeon him to death if it came to that.

He prowled about but Hawkins had fled. When he heard a horse galloping away, he knew Miranda was safe. Slocum turned around and finally stopped to stare at the crest of the next hill over in the cemetery. He had been there before. It was where Liam and Marie Neville had been buried alive. Trooping up the hill, he listened in the stillness and finally heard harsh breathing coming from an open grave.

Slocum walked past, then spun and fired double-handed as Hawkins rose from the grave. His bullet tore through the undertaker's gun hand. He yelped as the small pistol went flying. Eyes wide with fear, Hawkins looked up at him.

"Don't kill me, Slocum. Please, don't. I can give you money. More than you can spend in a lifetime. Please."

"Get out of the grave."

"Thank you, thank you." Hawkins scrambled up, bleeding hands high so Slocum wouldn't mistake his intent to surrender.

"Come on," Slocum said, motioning with Julian's pistol.

He rode back to the funeral parlor but Miranda had disappeared. Slocum decided she was going to do all right on her own since she had taken his advice about hightailing it. Riding back through Espero didn't appeal to him. He wanted nothing more than to be alone now. He turned his horse around and rode back down the road past the cemetery. He had just passed the iron arch over the entry to the graveyard when he heard hooves pounding hard behind him.

He drew rein and waited for Miranda to catch up.

"John, I'm glad I caught you before you rode off." She held the reins of another horse laden with burlap bags. "I had to go to the bank and get things Hawkins had stashed there. His brother objected, but not much." She handed him back his ebony-handled six-shooter.

He slid it into his empty holster. It felt good being armed again.

"I thought, me and you, we could ride together," Miranda said. "Harry's dead, and I know you won't do what we did and, well, you can steer me right."

Slocum laughed harshly at that.

"That's the first time anyone accused me of being a good influence." He looked at the heavily laden horse. "That what I think it is?"

"Hawkins owed it to me."

"That's everything he stole off the corpses?"

"Not everything. I would have needed a wagon for all of it, but it's what I could stash."

He considered her and what she carried. That much gold and silver was worth a fortune. More money than he would ever make in a lifetime.

"Either leave it and ride with me, or keep it and go your own way. I won't have any part of gold stolen off dead people."

"But, John, we're rich. You and me. Rich!"

He said nothing. It was her choice. Slocum snapped the reins and his horse walked off. He heard a loud crash as the burlap bags hit the ground. Miranda rode alongside him, her spare horse relieved of its load. She smiled, shook her head, and then said, "What happened to Hawkins?"

"You're going to have to put him behind you, too," Slocum said.

He looked to the top of the hill where a newly closed

grave stood—the grave alongside where Liam Neville had been buried alive. Although no breeze blew, the bell attached to a cord running into the coffin tinkled furiously.

"What's that?" Miranda asked. "It sounded like a gunshot, only muffled, far away."

"Nothing to worry about," Slocum said. He had left Julian's gun in the coffin with Hawkins. The undertaker had made his choice.

Slocum and Miranda picked up the pace and rode south out of Espero, heading for nowhere in particular as long as it was far, far away.

Watch for

SLOCUM AND THE REDHEADED DEVIL

425th novel in the exciting SLOCUM series
from Jove

Coming in July!